"Maybe ⏤ **bad-marriage gene,"** Liam said.

"I know the feeling."

"That's why you're still single?"

"One reason." The truth sat on the tip of Brooke's tongue, ready to be told. What was it about Liam that made her weaken her guard? She'd nearly opened up to him. She shook her head. No way did she know him enough to trust him. "It's my opinion that men cause destruction and ruin where ever they go."

"Funny, that's my opinion about women." His slow grin made her heart skip a beat.

Good thing her heart wasn't in charge. She was. And she wasn't going to let his stunning smile weaken her defenses any further.

"I know that's not fair." Liam winked. "But that's how it feels."

So hard to ignore that wink. She let it bounce off her, unaffected. She'd gotten as close to him as she was going to.

Best to remember she worked for him, she was leaving as soon as the trial was over and the last thing she wanted was a man to complicate things.

Books by Jillian Hart

Love Inspired

*A Soldier for Christmas
*Precious Blessings
*Every Kind of Heaven
*Everyday Blessings
*A McKaslin Homecoming
A Holiday to Remember
*Her Wedding Wish
*Her Perfect Man
Homefront Holiday
*A Soldier for Keeps
*Blind-Date Bride
†The Soldier's Holiday Vow
†The Rancher's Promise
Klondike Hero
†His Holiday Bride
†His Country Girl
†Wyoming Sweethearts
Mail-Order Christmas Brides
   "Her Christmas Family"
†Hometown Hearts
*Montana Homecoming

Love Inspired Historical

*Homespun Bride
*High Country Bride
In a Mother's Arms
   "Finally a Family"
**Gingham Bride
**Patchwork Bride
**Calico Bride
**Snowflake Bride

*The McKaslin Clan
†The Granger Family Ranch
**Buttons & Bobbins

JILLIAN HART

grew up on her family's homestead, where she helped raise cattle, rode horses and scribbled stories in her spare time. After earning her English degree from Whitman College, she worked in travel and advertising before selling her first novel. When Jillian isn't working on her next story, she can be found puttering in her rose garden, curled up with a good book or spending quiet evenings at home with her family.

Montana Homecoming
Jillian Hart

Love Inspired

Recycling programs
for this product may
not exist in your area.

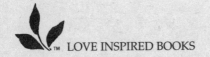

™ LOVE INSPIRED BOOKS

ISBN-13: 978-0-373-81618-7

MONTANA HOMECOMING

www.LoveInspiredBooks.com

Printed in U.S.A.

Trust in the Lord with all your heart.
—*Proverbs* 3:5

Chapter One

As Brooke McKaslin stepped foot outside onto the porch, a full moon peered over the stand of tall evergreens bordering the neighborhood. A touch of a chill hovered in the May evening. She slipped onto the top step and drew the edges of her cardigan sweater closed, remembering too late she was missing a button.

Night settled in a peaceful way. Somewhere a frog croaked from the ditch on the other side of the trees. Two or three streets over a car engine, in obvious need of a muffler, roared to life. Other than that, the neighborhood remained quiet. Golden light on curtained windows shone from nearby trailers where folks were cozy. She shifted on the step, as restless as she always felt when she came to Bozeman to visit.

It didn't help that her life was in turmoil. She'd just lost her job in Seattle because of cutbacks, leaving her financially strapped. Her stomach knotted at the inadequate amount in her savings account. Best not to think about that now. She'd come to Montana to lend her support to the family rallying around her younger sister, Brianna. Last year Bree had been critically injured in a violent robbery. A terrible time.

God had been gracious—Bree had survived and recovered fully. Now she would be a key witness for the prosecution in the upcoming trial. No one should go through that experience without family. Brooke's personal problems? They paled in comparison.

She breathed in the scent of lilacs from the bushes next door, drawing in the sweet, cool air. It felt good to have a moment to herself. She loved her family, but they wanted her to move to Montana permanently; they wanted her to put aside her past and be the girl they once knew.

Truth was? She did, too. The faint drone of the TV mumbled through the walls. She'd left her half sister, Colbie, and Colbie's mom, Lil, calling out questions to Alex Trebek's answers. No doubt they were still at it. She smiled, wishing she could have a regular life. That she could be that girl her family remembered, the one who believed in the good in people, the girl who had always known freedom.

Overhead stars glimmered like dreams far out of reach. She wondered how far away heaven was through the vast mystery of space. Did God see her sitting here worrying about her sister? She hoped He had heard her prayers.

Something crackled in the fenced yard next door. Twigs snapped. Bushes rustled. A bear tromping through underbrush couldn't make that much noise. Curious, she craned her neck to see if it was man or beast, but she couldn't see a thing. Just the tall fence and blooming lilacs.

"Oscar! Come back here," a man called. "Bad dog!"

His words held no sting but a hint of laughter as something scrabbled against the wooden fence. Paws appeared over the top followed by a snout and two short, floppy ears. A dog carrying something bulky in his mouth popped over the top rail and launched into the air.

"Oscar!" A dark head of hair bobbed on the other side of the fence boards. "Don't you dare run off!"

Brooke was on her feet before the dog's four paws hit the lawn. There was no other fence to slow down the escapee, not that a six-foot one had seemed to stop him. Although this neighborhood was quiet, a major road sat on the other side of the trees. That had to be hazardous for a dog on the loose.

"Here, boy." She held out one hand, running to intercept him. "Good, Oscar."

The yellow Lab spotted her, clutching something in his mouth. His surprised eyes glinted in the glow from the streetlight as he skidded to a halt in front of her. In a bid to change directions, his hind legs churned up grass and he bolted off down the middle of the road.

"Oscar!" A man landed with a two-footed thud in the flowerbed next to her. "Wow! That was close. I'm impressed. You almost had him."

"Almost doesn't keep him safe." She glanced over her shoulder at the trailer behind her, the door firmly closed. They were definitely alone. Shyness gripped her. "He went that way."

"Thanks." The man flashed a smile, glowing white in the deepening shadows. He dashed away, a tall, muscled athlete with brown hair and battered sneakers. That was all she noticed before he was lost in the darkness, his footsteps echoing.

Should she have run after the dog, too? She stared down at her combat boots. Not exactly running shoes. She wasn't athletic, either, at least not these days. Once she'd run cross-country and loved it, but then she'd loved a lot of things in life before they had been taken away. Before she had lost everything.

How could she help Oscar? The dog obviously didn't fear roads or cars. She bowed her head where she stood, clasped her hands and reached out in prayer. *Father, please let Oscar's owner catch him before any harm can come to him. Let there be a happy ending.*

When she opened her eyes and raised her head, she was sure the stars twinkled more brightly.

Did she hear the faint beat of paws against pavement? She tilted her head, straining her ears. Yes, thumping paws and heavy breathing were definitely coming her way. Oscar raced down the street toward her, galloping as hard as his four paws could carry him. His jaws stilled, stretched around something bulky clamped between his teeth.

"Oscar!" She took off, her boots clomping, but no way could she catch him. "Hot dogs! Cookies! Pizza!"

Words the dog knew. The Lab skidded to a stop, eyes wildly searching for what were any canine's favorite foods. She neatly wrapped her fingers around his collar. "Good boy, Oscar."

What looked and smelled like a baked ham dropped to the pavement as he hopped in place. Her arm jerked with his movements and her biceps burned trying to hold him. His teeth glistened in the half-light and excitement sizzled in his big brown eyes as if to say, "Oh, boy! Where's the pizza?"

"Good tactic." The dog owner's pleasant tenor rumbled close and his hand clasped the collar next to hers. "I'll have to remember that next time. Thanks for pitching in."

"Sure. I didn't want something bad to happen to him." Shyness seized her again. It was impossible not to notice the stranger's impressive height and the strong plane of his chest an inch from her shoulder, so she stumbled back a few steps where it felt safer and easier to breathe.

"Something bad is going to happen when my grandmother gets a hold of him." Amusement, not anger, laced his words. "He's going to be banned from the kitchen for months. Maybe forever."

"That's not surprising." She watched the stranger clip a leash to the collar and pat the dog's head. The Lab, obviously unconcerned with his disobedient ways, panted in appreciation, tongue lolling, before snatching his prize from the ground.

"I can't believe him." The tall guy shook his head. "He's not even sorry."

"Doesn't look like it since he's now eating the ham." She wrapped her arms around her middle, battling shyness. She was way out of practice when it came to guys. She'd worked in a women's halfway house for the past year. After what she'd been through, it seemed a good fit.

Men? They hadn't even been on her radar, not since her last boyfriend ruined her life nine long years ago. But something about this man drew her. Maybe it was his kindness as he gently wrestled the chunk of meat from the dog's mouth using not a single harsh or impatient word.

Definitely a nice guy. The faint glow from the streetlight gave an impression of high cheekbones, a straight nose and an unyielding line of a square jaw. He was gorgeous. Really gorgeous. That made her uncomfortable, too.

The neighbor's porch light came on and Mrs. Jones threw open her screen door.

"Did you catch that dog?" the elderly lady called out. "What about my ham?"

"I don't think you want it back, Gram." He held up the slobbery, half-eaten chunk. "It's a lost cause."

"I knew as much but I had to hold out hope." Mrs. Jones shook her head, clearly disapproving. "That was a good ham. I planned for the leftovers to last all week."

"I'll replace it."

"I told you that dog was more trouble than he was worth." A good-natured tone went along with those words. "You should take him back to that shelter. Make them return your money."

"Someone had to save him."

"It didn't have to be you." The door banged closed.

"Yes, it did." The handsome man trained his attention back to Brooke. "I decided my life was too boring so I visited the pound and took on a new adventure."

"It's good to see you're getting plenty of that.

And exercise, fresh air and a larger grocery bill." She willed her feet to move but they didn't. They remained stuck firmly to the ground and she had to wonder why.

Maybe it was simple curiosity. She wanted to see his smile in full light. The streetlamp overhead tried to illuminate him, casting a glow over his substantial height and broad shoulders and adding highlights to his brown hair. But his smile? It remained elusive in the shadows.

Why on earth was she wondering about some man? It was a total mystery.

"This is proof. You really have to beware what you pray for," he quipped, tucking the slobbery, half-devoured remains of the ham beneath his arm like a football. "I don't want you to get the wrong idea. I've only had Oscar two days. We're still getting to know each other and I'm finally figuring out the dog can't be trained."

"Sure he can." Brooke went down on both knees. As a farm girl, she was an animal lover from way back. "I've trained more than a few dogs in my day, so I know a great dog when I see one. You are it, Oscar."

At the sound of his name, the Lab leaped at her, licked her chin and danced in place. Probably remembering her earlier promises of cookies, hot dogs and pizza. "There's nothing wrong with his memory. I wish I had a cookie on me."

Both dog ears perked up. Brown eyes sparkled merrily as if to say, "Cookie? Where?"

"Oops, maybe I shouldn't have said that." She didn't have to search her pockets to know there wasn't anything she could offer in its place.

"It's okay. I have dog biscuits in my truck. C'mon, troublemaker." A few paces brought him to a big blue pickup sidled up close to Mrs. Jones's fence. The Lab's tail whipped back and forth as he bounded behind his owner. The truck door whispered open and after a little digging a bone-shaped treat appeared. The Lab lunged, clamped his teeth around the treat and crunched happily, crumbs raining from his mouth. His owner faced her. "You must be one of Colbie's sisters. You look a lot like her."

"I'm Brooke. I'm technically her older half sister."

"I'm Liam. I haven't seen you around before. I would have noticed."

She blushed. Had he just paid her a compliment? "Oh, I'm largely forgettable."

"I doubt that. Do you live around here?"

"Just visiting." She took a step backward, afraid her tongue would tangle any minute. A smart girl would escape while she could. When he gazed at her with piercing blue intensity, she felt smaller, aware of the past that haunted her. The past that would always stand between her and a normal life.

She lost who she'd been and she didn't know how to get that woman back. "How about you, Liam? Do you visit your grandmother often?"

"Whenever she can tempt me with good cooking." He had eyes the color of the sky at first light. The truest shade of blue she had ever seen. Dimples bracketed what was a picture-perfect smile. "How long will you be staying in town?"

"A couple of weeks, then it's back to Seattle."

His gaze brushed over her and her heart skipped a beat. The synapses in her brain ceased firing. Her feet lost contact with the pavement beneath her. Strange. Very strange.

"Oh, the trial. Of course." He snapped his free hand, the one not holding on tightly to the Lab's leash. The dog leaped up and down and pulled at his tether, scenting the air. "Oscar's looking for the ham. He's incorrigible."

"You're going to keep him, aren't you?" She inched close enough to stroke her fingers across the animal's soft head. She thought of the shelter, of caged doors and windowless walls, and shivered. She thought of no hope, no escape, no freedom. "You're not going to take him back to the pound?"

"No way. Gram was just joking. I hope." He patted his dog on the back. "Oscar's just a little excited, and I'm not exactly sure, but I don't think he's ever been left alone with a ham before. He lost his head and grabbed it before I could stop him. Next time he'll know better."

"Or run faster."

"A possibility." He chuckled. "Oscar catches on pretty quick. He likes you."

"Something tells me he likes everybody." A lock of dark hair tumbled across her face like a curtain, but it couldn't mask her beauty. She had a delicate heart-shaped face, deep violet-blue eyes and fragile features. She was petite, lost in the size-too-large sweater and jeans she wore. Brooke McKaslin reminded him of a spring dawn, so still a man might miss it entirely unless he really took the time to look.

When he did, nothing before had ever seemed as beautiful.

Funny he would take notice of her like this. The humiliation of his recent broken engagement normally kept him far away from most women. It was just plain crazy talking to this gorgeous woman. His shattered heart and crushed pride hadn't recovered from the last one. He'd been down that road, thanks. Not interested in going there again.

So why was he riveted by her? His heart rattled against his rib cage as he searched for an explanation and came up with nothing. A light flashed on and a screen door rasped open. Colbie McKaslin stood in the doorway, a worried frown on her face.

The sisters did look remarkably similar, with sleek dark hair and delicate faces, but he would never confuse the two. There was something innately amazing about Brooke, something that drew him whether he wanted to admit it or not.

"Oh, there you are!" Colbie called across the front yard. "*Jeopardy*'s over and I'm making cocoa. I thought you might want a cup, but I can see you're busy. Hi, Liam. Is that a dog?"

"It is." He took a few steps toward his truck, eager to go. "It's a long story."

"Didn't mean to interrupt. Sorry!" Colbie waved before she disappeared behind the closing screen door. Apparently she worried she'd interrupted a moment, but there wasn't one.

Not that he wasn't grateful to the lady for catching his dog.

"Oscar, you be a good boy." Brooke slipped away, nothing more than a faint outline in the shadows of the lawn. "Don't run from your master again."

At the sound of his name, the dog wagged his tail and hopped up and down, eager to race up to the pretty lady and follow her inside. She disappeared behind the screen door with nothing more than a final wave. The Lab whined, tipping his head side to side, not understanding why she had abandoned them.

"It's just you and me, buddy." He opened the back

door for the dog to jump up. "Come on, get in. Don't worry. Maybe our paths will cross hers again."

Thinking of tomorrow's trial, he had a feeling they might.

"So, you met Liam." Colbie closed the marshmallow bag with a rustle. "Isn't he a total wow?"

"I guess." Noncommittal, that was the best way to go. No doubt Colbie's well-meaning radar had ramped up to high. The last thing she wanted to do was to spend the rest of the evening discussing a man, especially when she was firmly, devotedly single.

"You *guess?*" Colbie's brows arched and she shook her head in disapproval. "I can't believe we're related. You can't tell me you don't notice gorgeous men when they happen to cross your path."

Brooke followed the aroma of steaming milk and dissolving cocoa powder into the kitchen, where three large mugs stood on the counter, topped with melting marshmallows. "I'm not looking for a man, gorgeous or otherwise. Are you?"

"Not especially. I'm thinking solely of you. You have to leave your possibilities open, sister dear." Colbie stuffed the bag into a pantry shelf, dark hair swinging. "You never know when true love will walk in and change your life."

"Or mess it up." She hid her smile as she chose a

mug and turned on her heel. "It's my opinion men cause wreck and ruin wherever they go."

"Some men. I can't argue that. But that's no excuse to turn into a spinster."

"A spinster? Isn't that like something out of the eighteen hundreds? There are no spinsters these days. Honestly." She strolled the short distance into the little living room and set the mug down on the end table within easy reach for Lil. "There's nothing wrong with being a woman in control of her life. Right, Lil?"

"Sorry, I can't help you, dear. I agree with Colbie." The pretty woman looked up from her wheelchair, her spirit bright in spite of the hardships life had dealt her. "Yes, a man can cause all sorts of havoc, but it all comes down to the kind of man he truly is deep inside. Seeing that inner truth of a man takes a lot of time and investment. Good men are hard to find, but they're out there. My prayer is that one of them finds you."

"Thanks, Lil, but save your prayers for Colbie." Brooke squeezed the hand of the sweet lady who was like a mother to her. "She needs them."

"I wouldn't mind a tall, dark, handsome hunk to stroll into my life." Colbie swept in carrying both mugs and set them on the coffee table. "On the other hand, he might get in the way of time spent with my mom, so maybe I'm better off without him."

"See my point?" Brooke dropped onto the couch and waited for her sister to plop down next to her. "Dudes change things. When it comes down to it, our lives are good. Who needs change?"

"My sentiments exactly." Colbie picked up the remote control and handed it to her mother. "Mom, your turn to pick. What are we going to watch?"

"Oh, you know I love that travel race show." Lil clicked a button and the screen flashed to a market scene in China. "I always meant to travel the world when I was you girls' age. I had such plans."

It wasn't just the wheelchair that had put a crimp in the woman's dreams. Sad, Brooke took a tentative sip of frothy cocoa, hot enough to nearly burn her tongue but good and sweet and comforting. She definitely needed the comfort. She knew what it was like to have life change suddenly and dreams evaporate. She blinked back images of a courtroom and the grim faces of a jury.

That dog had put a smile on her face tonight. She thought of Liam. He was so gorgeous. It was easy to picture him and Oscar trucking through the dark across town to wherever they lived. It would be easy to wish for a good man to love her. But that dream had been lost the moment the police had shown up at her door more than nine years ago. Life took you down paths you never imagined and all a person could do was deal with it. This was her dealing.

If her heart gave a little sigh over Liam she ignored it, counted her blessings and let the reality show carry her away.

Chapter Two

Liam headed down the sidewalk into the bright morning sun, feeling guilty at leaving his new dog home alone for the first time. He couldn't get the sound of Oscar's howl out of his head. Trying not to imagine how the poor dog was feeling, he focused on his work. The courthouse looming up ahead helped to remind him of his responsibilities.

He had to stop worrying. Oscar would be all right. He was safe in the house. Come five o'clock, Liam would walk back through that door and the dog would see he hadn't been abandoned. All would be well. Right?

Right.

"Oh, dear. Oops." A woman's good-natured trill caught his attention. He rounded the corner to see Lil in her wheelchair with her back to him, gazing down at her purse on the sidewalk.

"Hi, beautiful." He knelt to swoop up her leather

bag. "Don't you look fetching? You are going to turn heads in court today."

"Liam, you are a charmer." Lil accepted her handbag with a nod of thanks. "What good timing. Brooke, Colbie, look who I found walking the street."

"That makes me sound iffy. Like I'm up to no good."

"Oh, I suspect you are up to something very good." Lil's eyes twinkled merrily. "I hear you got yourself a dog."

"Guilty. It seemed like a good idea at the time. What can I say?" His few working brain cells decided to fail the moment Brooke circled around the back of the SUV and into sight. He opened his mouth intending to say something about Oscar but he forgot what.

Soft golden sunlight tumbled over her like a promise, glinting in sleek mahogany hair and caressing the curve of her delicately cut face.

Don't look, he instructed his brain, but his neurons didn't obey. Neither did his eyes, which could not stop taking her in. At first glance she seemed fragile, fine-boned, as if a brisk wind could carry her away. But when she leveled him with her hyacinth-blue gaze, an inner strength shone through, impressive and distinctive.

Wow. She'd been beautiful in the starlight, but

in the full day words failed him. Stunned, frozen, his jaw slack—did he look like a dolt?

Good thing he wasn't interested. Nope, not one bit. Her beauty bounced off him like rain on a roof. He remained unaffected.

"I hardly recognize you without your dog." Brooke didn't meet his gaze. "How is Oscar?"

"After making good on all your cookie promises, I sent him straight to bed with a new rawhide bone." He seized the grips of Lil's wheelchair, deciding to be useful.

"I'm glad to see you're handling him properly." She hiked the strap of her leather bag higher on her slim shoulder. She wore dress slacks and a solemn blouse and sweater, adding to her seriousness. What did he like about her most?

That was easy. She clearly gave him a "not interested" vibe. Not one thing about her hinted she might be open to further conversation with him. Not with the way she turned away, keeping her back to him.

This was a woman he could like. They were on the same wavelength.

"Come along, Lil." She ambled ahead, her tone softening with affection as she addressed the older woman. "Let's get you settled before the courtroom gets too busy."

"That would be easiest," Lil agreed cheerfully, tipping her head back to look up at him. A knowing grin made her sparkle. Multiple sclerosis might have put her in a wheelchair, but it hadn't slowed her down. "Do you know what you need, Liam?"

"I'm afraid to answer that question." He wasn't the dimmest bulb in the pack and he figured Brooke wasn't, either. The *tap-tap* of her heels could only be an attempt to escape Lil. Not that he blamed her. He gave the wheelchair a good shove to get it going. "What do I need? Maybe a haircut? A new attitude? A—"

"A dog trainer." Lil smiled as Brooke held the heavy courthouse door.

A dog trainer? He didn't see where she was going with this. A tiny zing at the back of his mind told him to be wary—there was something familiar but he couldn't place it. Mainly because all he could see was Brooke in full sunlight. Her ivory complexion, her chiseled, fine-boned features and her full, rosebud mouth. Why couldn't he look away?

"Don't do it, Lil." Brooke rolled her eyes as a breeze of wind rustled the ends of her dark hair. "Don't condemn me to that."

"To what?" Then it hit him. He remembered her gentle touch, how the Lab had taken to her, that she had been the one to catch the runaway. So, the pieces were all starting to fit. He guided the wheelchair into the busy lobby.

"You need help with that dog, young man." Lil

glimmered like a rare gem. "Brooke, you've trained how many dogs?"

"Not many," Brooke hedged as she fell in line behind him at the security checkpoint. "Hardly any at all."

"She's modest." Lil's words held a mother's love. "She grew up on a farm outside Miles City. She's been around animals all her life. 4-H, all the good stuff. She won more blue ribbons than a body can count for her animals at the county and state fairs. She trained all the family's herding dogs. I think she would be able to handle one mischievous yellow Lab."

"Please, Lil. Stop." She rolled her eyes. "That was a long time ago. I'm sure if Liam wants to find a dog trainer, then he's more than capable of finding one on his own."

"Maybe. Maybe not." His stunning blue eyes met hers and held, full of trouble and a glint of quiet humor. He did not look like a man upset by Lil's meddling. The woman was clearly trying to match her up with Mr. Handsome. "I do have a dog in need of training. I don't know where to start. Some folks would hire a trainer in this exact situation."

"There are plenty of good obedience schools in the area, I'm sure."

"But Brooke, honey, I thought you could use the work." Lil's caring was hard to turn down.

"Oh." She felt foolish. Lil had been trying to help with her precarious financial position.

"Look, there's Colbie." Pleased, Lil clasped her hands together. "Did you find a parking spot close in, dear?"

"Would I be out of breath if I had?" Colbie laughed raggedly as she broke away from security. She seemed to bring the sunshine with her. "Liam, thanks for piloting Lil, but I'll take over."

"I don't know. You know I'm sweet on Lil. I might have to keep her."

"Too bad. You'll have to fight me for her." With a wink, Colbie wrapped her hands around the grips and gave the wheelchair a practiced shove toward courtroom five. "Are you ready, copilot?"

"I'm ready, captain." Lil's amusement lingered after she and Colbie headed down the busy corridor.

Leaving her and Liam alone.

Maybe she hadn't been completely wrong about Lil's motives. She squinted at the man beside her. Tall, thick dark hair, granite face, rugged features, handsome enough to give most women in a five-mile radius butterflies.

Not her, but most women.

"Looks like they don't need a navigator." What was she going to do about Liam? And what exactly were the chances of running into him two days in a row? "What you are doing at the courthouse? Wait, don't tell me. You're here for a trial."

"You mean a trial of my own?"

"Sure. You don't strike me as a thief, but I've learned you can't judge a book by its cover." She tried to keep her tone light, easygoing, just making conversation as she walked down the corridor. But the truth? She felt the pain of her past and the walls closing in. The courthouse brought back too many memories. "You never know what's inside."

"Funny. With me, what you see is what you get." He winked at her, shortening his gait to match hers. "Well, most of the time. I don't have secrets."

"Everyone has secrets." Secrets. Her secrets whispered until the past was all she could see. "You're being evasive."

"Me? I'm not the evasive sort." That grin of his could make a girl's neurons fail completely.

Fortunately not hers. She was immune to a man's charm, thanks to her last boyfriend, Darren. "Then why are you at the courthouse early on a Monday morning?"

"I'm not a thief and, no, I'm not a lawyer. Although if I'd chosen differently, I might have been one. Both of my parents are, they're off in L.A., and that's what they expected me to be. A summer volunteering in Ecuador changed that."

"You volunteered?" She raised one eyebrow. This man with his magazine-cover polish, perfect black suit and patterned tie? With a briefcase clutched in one hand? "Wait, don't tell me. Probation?"

"Funny." His chuckle was as warm as she might have expected. "I volunteered as part of my church's youth group. We stayed in a village that had no electricity or running water. We worked to put in a water system and irrigation for crops. I liked it so much I volunteered every summer until I was out of college. Because I had to work for a living, I decided to stick closer to home with my volunteer efforts."

"I'm not impressed." Fine, maybe a little. But she didn't have to admit that out loud.

"Didn't expect you to be." Dimples played at the corners of his smile. "Let me guess. You've done a lot of volunteering, too. Animal shelters?"

"Yes. Good guess." She hesitated, not knowing how to explain. She felt akin to those animals forgotten in cages. She'd lost so much of her life after Darren's betrayal and her trial, and she'd lost herself, too. Helping in the city shelter gave her the chance to make a difference and to work with animals, something she'd always wanted to do with her life. "I put in a lot of time at the shelter close to where I lived. I was there so often, I knew every animal by name."

"Busy? That on top of a job has to keep you hoppin'."

His voice dipped low, interested.

"At times." Uncomfortable, she shrugged. She didn't try to explain. A man like him, so polished and confident, would never understand. What did he see when he looked at her? She gave her thrift-store sweater a tug. "I like to keep busy."

"Busy is good," he agreed.

She risked another sideways glance at him. Strong profile, thick dark hair, a straight nose, square-cut chin, a man who radiated a quiet integrity that anyone would believe in. But did she?

"Volunteering keeps me out of trouble."

"Oh, sure. Me, too."

"You volunteer still?"

"Guilty. I can't help myself."

They shared a smile. She could read in his eyes the truth, the same truth she couldn't say aloud. There was true need in this world. She'd never been able to turn her back on it. Neither could he.

"See?" His smile deepened, making his dimples irresistible. "We're more alike than you first thought. We stand on common ground."

"Maybe a tile or two," she quipped, feeling uneasy again because the lights in his blue irises shone genuinely, with no falseness.

Everyone hid things, she reminded herself before she could start to believe him. Everyone had places within them they kept secret. Buried disappointments, shortcomings, failures. She swallowed hard, looking at the yawning doors, fighting the trace of panic setting in.

She hadn't been in a courthouse since her trial. This was a different place, but the sounds were the same. The buzz of conversation echoing in the corridor, the tap of her shoes on the cold white tile, the cavernous seriousness that wrapped around her like a tomb. Trying not to remember, she played with the hem of one sweater sleeve, seeing in her mind the judge's bench, the witness box and the empty chairs for the jury. She blinked hard until the memory faded.

"Brooke McKaslin? Is that you?" An aggressive woman tore through the crowd. A brown, curly cap of hair, assessing eyes and a cat's grin locked on her. "Tasha Brown with Action News. Tell me, how does it feel to step foot in this courtroom?"

A reporter. Shock rocked her back on her heels. She hadn't prepared for this. She despised reporters, always digging up dirt and thriving on it. Why did someone have to unearth it now? It happened so long ago. The shame of the past struck her hard. She gasped, fisted her hands, lost sight of the doorway. Her vision blurred.

"No comment." The words squeaked out of her, full of pain. But did the reporter stop?

No. The woman jabbed her handheld recorder closer. "Your family isn't any stranger to courthouses. First your father—"

"Excuse me," she interrupted, unable to see a way out. People surrounded her in every direction, closing in to get to the courtroom. Panic raced through her veins. She couldn't breathe. There just wasn't any air. And how could she escape? She was trapped by people everywhere.

A steady hand clasped around her elbow. Liam. Strong but gentle. The comfort of his touch reminded her she wasn't alone.

Over the whir of panic she heard the resonate rumble of his voice, keeping the reporters at bay. He tugged her close to the wall and blocked her with his body.

"Thank you." She drew in a ragged breath, feeling a little foolish. She definitely felt wrung out.

"No problem," he answered kindly. "I—"

"There you are!" Colbie burst into sight like a fish swimming against the current, weaving around people filing into the chamber. Her violet eyes shone with caring. "Court is about to start. C'mon."

Brooke felt her sister's unspoken sympathy wrap around her like a hug. Colbie understood. Colbie who had so faithfully written letters all those years when Brooke had been away, cut off from life, behind barred doors and windowless walls.

Lord, help me to do this. She gathered all the strength she had. She could walk into that court-room, sit beside her sisters and ignore the reporters. She was strong and tough. Not once would she remember being perched in her chair beside a defense attorney with her world in tatters. Colbie's hand slipped around hers as Liam let go.

She turned to him at a loss, unsure what to say. He'd witnessed her panic attack, the remnants of which were still quaking through her. But did he ask questions? No. Kindness softened his deep eyes and made him amazing.

Just amazing.

With Colbie's hand in hers, she set her chin, squared her shoulders and walked into the courtroom as if the past had no claim on her.

At times his fellow colleagues miffed him, and it burned through the morning session. Liam sat in the back where he could watch the entire courtroom, not that there was much going on other than opening arguments and preliminaries. He was on assignment, so he was interested in the case but he had a hard time concentrating. He could still hear Brooke's gasp of pain at Tasha Brown's question. Interrogating family members outside the courtroom. He clenched his jaw, hands fisting.

Fine, so he felt protective of Brooke. He would respond the same way toward anyone in a similar situation. And if a little voice in the back of his head wanted to argue, he simply ignored it.

She hadn't glanced his way once all morning. He

had a perfect view of her, seated with her family down front. They nestled together in an unbreakable circle around Brianna. Brooke's sleek dark hair glinted in the lights, and he remembered the feel of her arm, fine-boned and soft beneath his hand. Asking her for a quote hadn't even occurred to him. Why had Tasha done it?

The Backdoor Burglars had been big news a while back, before he'd moved back home. Thieves had preyed on restaurants when employees were cleaning up for the night. The robberies escalated until several people were killed and more were injured. He'd been out of the country, but his grandfather Ed Knightly had covered the series of crimes. A real tragedy.

He recognized Juanita's family, a young woman killed in the robbery, her mother teary-eyed and trying to stay strong.

"Hey, Liam." Roger, a fellow journalist, interrupted his thoughts. "Want to grab lunch?"

He blinked, realizing the session had adjourned for noon recess. He hadn't even noticed it. Some reporter he was. He tucked his notes and laptop into his briefcase. "Sorry, can't. I've got to buzz home and check on my dog."

"You have a dog?" Roger's eyebrows arched in surprise. *"You?"*

"Hey, what's wrong with me?" He eased off the bench. "I'm a good dog owner."

"Yeah, but you are gone a lot. Won't that be a problem?"

"Why would it? Oscar used to spend his time locked in a cage, and now he has a whole house. Where's the problem in that?"

He got ahead of the crowd streaming toward the doors, catching one quick glimpse of Brooke. She bent to speak to Lil, dark hair cascading over her shoulder, strain tightening the muscles along her delicate jaw line. The trial was obviously taking a toll on her. It was a lot for a family to go through.

"Hey, maybe there's no problem. What do I know?" Roger kept pace with him as they broke out into the wide corridor. Noise and people streamed around them. "My mom had a dachshund, and that little wiener dog ate the entire house whenever she left him alone. That's all I'm saying."

"The only danger would be if Oscar ever learned how to open the fridge or the pantry doors." He thought of the ham incident and grinned. That dog was sure livening things up. "See you in an hour."

"Right. Good luck!"

"I don't believe in luck." God had led him to Oscar, God had put the wish for a dog into his heart and God would not abandon him now. Liam headed down the hall, glancing over his shoulder to steal another glimpse of Brooke. The crowd was too big—he couldn't see her. He stumbled out the door and into the bright May sunshine, fighting the feeling he'd left something important behind.

His cell sang a cheerful note as he started his truck's engine. One glance at the screen had him grinning. It was a text message from Colbie.

Mom told me about your need for a dog trainer. Brooke is great with dogs, she'd written. Call her, text her, just don't hire anyone else. Promise?

I don't need a trainer, he tapped out with his thumbs. His dog was unruly but overall just fine. And on the off chance Colbie was playing matchmaker, he didn't need that, either. He knew how to hold his ground.

Famous last words, Colbie wrote. I'm sending Brooke's cell # anyway.

The drive home was quick and uneventful. He lived in an older section of Bozeman where the neighborhoods were tree-lined and straight out of the 1940s with white picket fences, carefully manicured yards and Craftsman-style homes. He parked in front of the detached garage, hopped up the back steps and turned his key in the lock. The ringing bark of welcome put a spring in his step as he swung open the kitchen door.

A golden streak launched toward him, emitting a high-pitched whine of relief. Eighty pounds of Lab hit him in the chest, rocking him back on his feet. Paws settled on his shoulders, his knees gave way and he stumbled as the dog plastered canine kisses across his face.

"I'm glad to see you, too, buddy. Now, down." Laughing, he grabbed two paws and lifted them off his suit jacket, wiped his face with his sleeve and pushed through the door.

That's when he saw the kitchen. Disaster. Air squeaked out of his lungs in shock. He blinked, but the scene remained. Trash littered the tile, the garbage can overturned and empty. One ladder-back chair remained in place at the small nook table, but the other three sprawled on their backs in various places around the room. One was missing a leg.

"You ate part of a chair?" He jammed one hand through his hair, too stunned to do anything more than stare. Cushions had been torn off the chairs and were almost intact with white flashes of stuffing showing. One cupboard door hung askew.

"I can't believe this." He shook his head, stunned by the devastation. A mini tornado could not have left as much damage. "Oscar, how could you?"

The Lab whined and sat on his haunches. Doggy brows furrowed sorrowfully. Big chocolate-brown eyes beamed a message that seemed to say, "Forgive me. I was bad."

"Oh, Oscar." Liam rubbed the pounding tension settling in behind his left temple. How could he be mad at that face? He could only hope the rest of the house hadn't suffered the same fate.

Chapter Three

"How are you holding up?" Her big brother Luke leaned in to ask, his voice so low it was difficult to hear him in the bustling sandwich shop.

"Fine." All morning she'd endured sympathetic looks and comforting hugs and encouraging smiles from her family, but no one had said the words aloud. Pain clamped around her ribs. Her hands shook as she dug in her purse for a couple of twenties to help pay for the family meal.

"I've got it," her oldest brother, Hunter, grumbled, standing in front of her in line. He fished a credit card from his wallet. "Put your money away, Brookie."

"I should at least pay for my own sandwich."

"Not going to happen." Hunter was used to being in charge. As the oldest son, he'd borne the brunt of their father's failures. Their youngest brother's death had been the last straw. Hunter had grown harder through the years until it was almost impossible to remember the laughing, good-humored boy he'd been. They had been The Three Musketeers, she and Luke and Hunter roaming the hills and fields on their family's land. Those long-ago happier times felt far away.

"You don't look fine." Luke's voice turned gruff, another strong man uncomfortable showing his caring side. "You haven't looked fine since you stepped foot inside the courtroom door this morning."

"I don't want to talk about it." She'd meant to sound firm, but her voice came out strangled. The memories were a noose tightening around her throat, one she could not loosen.

"Leave her be, Lucas," Hunter grumbled as he handed his card across the narrow counter to a smiling clerk in a green apron. "We all know life isn't fair. No sense in dragging all that up again."

Relief filtered through her, loosening the imaginary noose enough so she could breathe. All her life Hunter looked out for her, taking care of her, both he and Luke.

"I didn't mean to drag up any bad stuff." Luke's brawny arm slid around her shoulders, hooked her by the neck and gave her a brief brotherly one-armed hug. "Just trying to help."

"Stop helping." Hunter shook his head and dug cash out of his pocket for the tip jar. A hint of a grin hooked the corners of his stern mouth. Growly on the outside, soft on the inside. "Go fill the cups, would you, Brookie?"

"Some things never change no matter how long you are away." She shook her head, also fighting to hide a smile. "Bossy, bossy, bossy."

"Someone has to be in charge. Why not me?" Hunter quipped as she grabbed the stack of cups on the counter.

"Why does it always have to be you?" Luke good-naturedly argued, his voice trailing after her as she headed for the soda machines.

Her brothers' banter faded into indistinct rumbles blending with the other conversations in the busy shop. In their way, her brothers were trying to help and she loved them for it. She extracted one cup from the stack and stabbed it beneath the ice dispenser, and the anxious knot in her middle eased a notch. She had been away from home too long. She missed them all so much.

"Looks like you could use some help." Colbie sidled in to steal two cups from the stack. "Brianna seems to be holding up well. It can't be easy to have to relive what happened to her that night."

"No, I'm sure it's not." She feared her sharp-eyed half sister's comment had a double meaning, that Colbie was also gently wondering the same about Brooke. She closed the door on her memories, leaving them buried. She filled the cup with root beer, glancing over her shoulder. Bree and her identical twin, Brandi, sat at a table near Lil. Bree's handsome fiancé towered at her side, his strong arm around her as if determined to protect her from the world.

Nice. She was so grateful her sister had found someone to love her, someone honest and good. Brianna deserved a happy future.

Her phone erupted into an electronic tune, surprising her. Who could it be? Root beer sloshed over the rim and onto her knuckles as she clapped on a plastic lid. Most people who would call her were in this restaurant. She thought of the applications she'd sent out before boarding the bus in Seattle. Oh, what if it was someone about a job?

"I'd better get this." She opened her bag, heart pounding, fingers fumbling. *Please, let it be a good job,* she prayed.

"You go ahead. I'll finish up." Colbie shooed her away with an encouraging grin.

A little swish of hope beat through her as she stepped away. All she needed was a job to get back on her feet—that was all. Just one job. Any job. Her former position hadn't paid well, but it had included her room and she didn't need much to get by. She found her phone by feel in the bottom of her bag and checked the number.

Not an out-of-area phone call, she saw from her phone's screen, but Liam Knightly's name. He'd sent her a picture. Odd. She hit a button and a vivid image of a living room popped onto the display. Her jaw dropped at the image in full Technicolor. She stared unblinking at a living room in complete disarray. The couch had no cushions, lamps were toppled and DVDs were scattered all over the floor. Had he been robbed?

Wait a minute. She remembered a certain yellow Lab and the ham incident. Had Oscar done this? A grin stretched across her face. She couldn't help it. That dog could sure destroy a room. Clearly a natural talent, poor boy.

Another chime, another picture. This one appeared to be of a spare bedroom made into an office. A desk's empty surface shone beneath a sunny windowsill, a printer, a telephone and paper lay on the floor surrounding it. One closet door hung lopsided off its frame. In the corner of the room sat a yellow dog on an overstuffed chair, front paws propped on one chewed-up arm, a deliriously happy grin on his canine face.

"That's a cute dog." Colbie glanced over her shoulder. "Why did he do that to the room?"

"Separation anxiety. How did Liam get my number?"

"It's a mystery." Eyes sparkling, Colbie sashayed away loaded down with soda cups.

It was no mystery at all. Brooke rolled her eyes. A text message filled her screen.

I need professional help, Liam wrote.

That's a private matter between you and your therapist. Her thumbs flew across the keys.

Funny. Just what I need. A comedic dog trainer.

She huffed out a breath. I'm not a dog trainer.

Colbie said U were.

She sighed. Colbie is a meddler.

That doesn't change the fact I need a dog trainer. U interested?

The image of his face, of the amused, easygoing gleam in his striking blue eyes, came to her as easily as if he stood in front of her. Definitely a bad sign and a hint that maybe she should turn down his job offer.

But, come to think of it, she could use the work. Clearly Oscar could use some help adjusting to his new home. Her thumbs tapped out an answer. Maybe.

I'll pay whatever U want. His words seemed frantic. Just help me.

I'm not sure U can be trained, but I can try.

Me? What about Oscar?

For his sake, I'll do it. She hit Send, shaking her head. So, she had a job of sorts after all.

Her phone chimed with Liam's next text. Great. Whew. I need your help desperately.

With a little training up, I think you will make a fine dog owner, she typed and hit Send.

"I haven't seen you smile like that in a decade."

Hunter ambled up, carrying two loaded trays of sandwiches. "Got a boyfriend we don't know about?"

"He's not even a friend and that's the way it will stay, so don't look at me like that."

"Like what?"

"Like you know something I don't." Brothers. She grabbed the rest of the sodas and joined her brother at the two tables the family had claimed. After she handed out the drinks, her cell chimed again.

Me? I don't need training. I already know how to sit. How to fetch.

She could imagine the manly crinkles in the corners of Liam's eyes as he grinned, typing those words. She eased into a chair, tapping out an answer on the keys. It's a start. Text me your address and I'll swing by after court.

"Brooke, we're waiting on you to say grace." Hunter frowned as if annoyed as he stacked the emptied trays. His annoyance was pure show. His dark gaze shone with gentleness.

"Oops." She stuffed her phone into her bag and bowed her head as Hunter began the prayer. She added silent thanks for her blessings of family and a plea for poor Oscar. If things didn't work out, she would hate for him to go back to living behind barred doors. She shivered, breaking a little inside at the memory. She knew exactly how heartbreaking that existence could be.

Squinting against the late afternoon sun shining in her eyes, she pulled to a stop at the curb. The small pickup she'd borrowed from Brianna idled roughly as she put it in Park.

This was Liam's house? She studied the bungalow shaded by two broadleaf maples. The front porch framed two spacious windows and a front door, giving the home a smiling look.

A bark erupted the moment she opened the truck's door. A golden blur streaked across the tidy lawn as she rose to her feet.

"No, Oscar! No!" Liam's laughter held no sting as his command echoed in the front yard. He raced into sight but not fast enough to stop the golden blur from springing over a row of low shrubbery.

She caught sight of ears up, tongue lolling and bright canine eyes gleaming. She braced for impact, just in case. "Oscar, sit."

Did it work? Not a chance. Paws hit her shoulders, a tongue swiped from her chin to her forehead and she sat down hard on the sidewalk, eighty pounds of dog in her lap.

"Brooke, are you all right?" Liam's concern, Liam's hand on her arm, his caring blue eyes meeting hers.

"I'm fine." A dog's happy kiss swiped across her

face again and she laughed. Really laughed. After a hard day dealing with ghosts of her past and worries of how the trial was affecting Brianna, Oscar's exuberance felt like a gift, a true blessing that was as welcome as the warm May sun and the song of the breeze through the maple leaves. "Oscar, you are a great boy. Do you know that?"

Chocolate eyes twinkled a happy answer. The big dog leaped and danced on the sidewalk, caught a whiff of her purse and tried to stick his nose beneath the leather flap.

"Oscar?" Liam caught his collar. "No more destruction. You've maxed out your daily limit, buddy."

"I think he's going for the dog biscuits I picked up on the way over. It seemed like a good idea at the time."

"Careful. Leather is edible, at least to him. So are most materials known to man." He held out his free hand to help her from the ground. She reached without thought, her palm sliding against his. A jolt of awareness whispered through her, the oddest of sensations, a charged sweetness. What on earth? She'd never experienced anything like that before.

Did he feel this, too? She couldn't tell. His face remained unchanged as his hand fell away from hers, leaving her palm tingly. Somehow she made her feet work, falling into stride beside him. Oscar bounded between them on the walkway, sniffing her purse.

"How is Brianna holding up?" Kindness layered Liam's question. "This had to be a hard day of remembering."

"Yes, but she's awesome. She's been through a lot of trauma but she's handling this better than I could in her shoes."

"Have she and Max set a wedding date yet?"

"Word is they want a Christmas wedding, although nothing official yet." She tapped up the front steps and onto the cozy porch, keeping a good hold on her bag. Oscar had begun to drool. "They are going to wait until all this court stuff is over."

"Smart. Finish one chapter, then start another." He pulled open the front door, giving her a new view of the destruction. "I haven't been home long enough to tackle this."

"Oh, Oscar." She gaped at the scene. The pictures Liam sent hadn't begun to tell the whole story. Amazed, she walked into the ruin, stepping over DVD cases and fluffs of stuffing from the couch pillows, shocked at Oscar's thoroughness.

The Lab whined, worry furrowing his doggy brow.

"You know that was wrong, don't you?" She kept her voice gentle but didn't hide her disappointment in him.

Oscar's head sank. His haunches went down. No whine had ever sounded as sorry.

"See? This is my problem." Liam's gaze speared hers, full of sympathy for his canine friend. "He loses his head and then regrets it later. He's not a bad dog."

"Not even close." She liked Liam more for understanding that. With the slant of the light through the windows falling across him he appeared gilded, like a dream. Why did her heart skip three beats? Why couldn't she pull away to put more physical distance between them?

All good questions. The fact that she actually felt a little comfortable with him surprised her more. Maybe it was how he'd protected her earlier in the courtroom corridor, hauling her purposefully away from the nosy reporter. She wasn't good at letting anyone do something for her, even family. She'd become very self-reliant. Maybe too self-reliant. His help had felt nice.

Liam gave the front door a push, closing it with a final click. He squared his shoulders as he surveyed the room. "I've been wanting to redecorate anyway."

Funny. She liked that about him, too. The left side of his mouth crooked upward into a grin and a dimple dug into his lean cheek. Totally a likeable guy.

"Do you know what you need?" She did her best to drag her gaze away from his riveting dimple.

"A swift kick for my brilliant idea to get a dog?"

"No, because it *was* a brilliant idea. You saved him. You gave him a new life." She tried to sound casual, keeping her approval tucked down deep. Did she succeed? Who knew? She suspected probably not. "What you need is someone to help you clean up this mess."

"You would do that?" Liam's gaze harpooned her and she could see into him, where his kindness lived.

"Why not?" She wasn't affected by him. Really. And that was the story she was sticking with. "I like to help where I can, and let's face it, you have a problem here. It's hard to believe one dog could do so much damage."

"Wait till you see the kitchen." The dimple cutting into his cheek deepened and so did the gleam in his eyes. "That's nice of you, Brooke. It's the best offer I've had all day."

"Probably the only offer you've had all day."

"True." His chuckle rumbled smooth and warm like butter melting, and a matching dimple bracketed the right corner of his mouth. For most women that would probably be irresistible.

Good thing she was immune.

"I may as well feed you since you're here anyway." A casual invitation as he knelt to gather up a bunch of DVD cases. Most of them only had a few teeth marks. "I've got some meat defrosting in the kitchen. All I can offer you is a hamburger."

"I've never met a hamburger I haven't liked."

"Excellent. Another thing we have in common."

"You're counting?" She rescued a couch cushion from the floor.

"Just making conversation. Trying to figure out the puzzle that is Brooke McKaslin."

"I'm a puzzle?"

"Only in that I don't know anything about you." He set the DVDs on a shelf. "I've known Colbie and Lil for years, ever since they moved in next door to my grandmother. We attend the same church."

"Then why didn't I see you at yesterday's service?" She studied him with an analytical arch to her amazing blue eyes and it made his heart catch.

That lurch in his chest bothered him.

"Let me guess." He rescued more DVDs from the floor. "You went to the early service."

"And you didn't?"

"Nope. I find it tough to get up early on Sunday."

"Ah, another piece of the puzzle that is Liam Knightly."

"I'm no puzzle. With me, what you see is what you get."

"That's too bad."

He rolled his eyes, laughing along with her. He

rescued a few stray DVDs that still might work once the dried slobber was cleaned off. He gave them a swipe with his sleeve. "So, what do you do besides coming to the rescue of desperate dog owners?"

"I'll let you know. I'm currently unemployed."

"Ouch. Been there." He matched up DVDs with their mangled cases, but where were his eyes? Watching her. "It was long, long ago but I remember it clearly. Unemployment is not fun."

"No, but I'm not dwelling on it. Something will work out." She straightened the last cushion. Her movements, graceful and self-conscious, stole him. It was as if she'd reached right over and tried grabbing his heart.

"Well, something worked out for you today. Oscar is your next job." He swallowed against the tightness in his throat, but nothing could dispel the odd sensation of almost being caught by her.

He didn't want to be caught by anyone.

"I'm sure Oscar will be the best job I've ever had. He's a sweetie."

"I'm glad you think so." He ambled around the coffee table, still on its side, and bent to right it. "Colbie might keep finding you work."

"You never know. She's certainly determined." She dug in her purse and withdrew a packet of needles and different-colored thread bobbins. "I think she wants me to find something here so that I'll stay in Montana."

"Do you want to stay?" He heaved the oak coffee table onto all four legs, watching her through his lashes.

"I don't know." Her voice dipped. "I've gotten used to life in Seattle."

"Oh, I get it. You have someone there. A boy-friend?" Why was he disappointed? He should not be bummed because Brooke had a significant other.

"No, no way. Just a life I've gotten comfortable with." She held up a length of thread to one of the couch cushions, nodded and chose a needle.

No boyfriend? Why was he relieved? "Some-times you have to step out of your comfort zone. Take a risk."

"I've done that. Got burned." She shrugged, oddly vulnerable and trying to hide it. "Lived to regret it. Hugely."

"Who hasn't?"

"True." He didn't know what it was about her that drew him. It was a mystery he had to figure out. Was it her honesty, like the quietest note of a hymn, that hooked him? Or the promise of an amazing spirit that went along with her breath-stealing beauty? He wished he knew. One thing he liked was a puzzle. It was the reporter in him.

He had to know more, so he tried again. "What do you do for a living?"

"A little of this, a little of that." She threaded the needle. "I think the couch cushion is totally salvageable, but what about that throw pillow?"

"Not a chance of saving it, and I'm the one asking the questions." He swept up the pillow missing half its stuffing. He had more pressing matters, mainly the intrigue of Brooke McKaslin. "Where did you go to college?"

"I didn't."

Curious. He would have pegged her for an intellectual type with a degree in fine arts or maybe social work. She stayed away for most holidays or he would have spotted her at Gram's long before this. "Why did you move so far from your family?"

"Uh…" She looked up from knotting her thread. Her long hair whipped as she glanced around the room. "Liam, where is Oscar?"

"Nice one, but you aren't going to distract me. I'm on a mission—"

"No, really, where's Oscar?" Concern tugged at her rosebud lips. "Where did he go?"

A crash rang from the kitchen, accompanied by the thud of something four-footed landing on the floor. A plate clattered to a ringing stop.

"Mystery solved," Liam quipped. "He's in the kitchen helping himself to our dinner."

Chapter Four

"Amazing. The wrapping isn't even stopping him." Liam surveyed what remained of the defrosting pound of hamburger with disbelief etched on his face. "Worse, it didn't even slow him down."

"Oscar has a gift, that's for sure." Brooke laughed. "Oscar, give."

Recognition sparked in chocolate-brown eyes. The dog obviously knew the word. His jowls stopped working. Big, sharp teeth clamped mutinously. With his big feet braced and every muscle tensed, he did not want to relinquish his prize.

"Oscar." She willed a little authority into her voice. "Give."

His eyes went down. His head went down. With one big swallow he gulped the rest of the meat before there was any hope of recovering it. All she saw was a flash from the wrapping paper before it disappeared behind his sharp teeth.

"I'm disappointed in you." She let that show in her words, too.

Oscar swallowed one final time and whined in defeat, and his nose drooped to the floor as if he were disappointed in himself, too. Doggy brows arched in dismay.

A perfect picture of remorse.

"Just like with the ham." Liam raked his fingers through his thick locks of hair. "He totally lost his head and lived to regret it."

"We'll have to work on his impulse control. And you." She whirled at him, doing her best not to notice the concern for the dog on his face, the fact that he wasn't angry, that he wasn't quick to lash out at the dog. "You know he has food issues. You shouldn't have left that meat out to tempt him."

"Me? *I'm* in trouble?" He chuckled at that, thought about it, shook his head. "I probably deserve it. You're right. I clearly need training."

"Glad you can admit it. That's the first step." She shouldn't be chuckling along with him. Just like she shouldn't be noticing how handsome he was with his silk tie askew and loosened, with his striped dress shirt a little wrinkled and the top button undone. She shouldn't be noticing the way the sunlight backlit him, glossing him like a statue. The most incredible statue she'd ever seen—sculpted masculine features, carved muscled physique and compassion towering over her.

Don't gasp. Don't stare. Don't notice. She swallowed hard, trying to will her eyes to move away from him. Did they?

No. Did she want them to?

No. And wasn't that the problem? Surely if she tried hard enough she could talk herself into it, right?

"I've got to get used to having you around, buddy." He knelt to rub the dejected dog's head. Poor Oscar was so unhappy with himself, he whined even harder. Worry creased his canine face. "We'll figure it out, yes we will. I'm guessing you were awful hungry at least one time in your life, huh, buddy?"

"He probably was." Brooke knelt, caught by the man's sensitivity, impressed that he'd figured out what was driving Oscar's behavior on a deeper level. "Everyone has things that motivate them or hold them back. Even dogs."

"Are you telling me he's always going to be a food thief?" Humor in those words, sympathy for Oscar in those deep eyes.

"It's likely. He'll get better, but it's easier to train you not to leave food out."

"Ah, that's what you meant about the training me thing?"

"Sorry, Liam, but that's only the tip of the iceberg. You are going to require a lot of training before you deserve this guy." Laughing, seeking refuge in humor instead of her feelings, she brushed her fingertips across the soft fur of Oscar's neck.

Relief squeaked through the dog's tight-sounding throat. His tongue lashed out, swiping across her face one, two, three times so fast she could barely pull away as the fourth one hit her. Raw ground beef dog breath. She shook her head. All part of the job. "I say you should feed this guy. Don't waste any time. Where's his kibble?"

"Look around." Liam swept his hand to the floor, where pieces of dried dog food were scattered over the entire span of the linoleum. It had been flung under the lip of the cabinets, tossed into the corners and tucked beneath the debris of what was once an organized kitchen.

"Oscar." The pictures hadn't told the full story. Everything had been knocked off the counters. Even the magnets from the refrigerator's front panel. "You're a nut. You know that?"

Oscar's single bark reverberated through the kitchen, just short of deafening. He looked happy to be understood at last.

"What about us?" Liam tugged open the pantry door and unrolled the food bag. Oscar's ears went up. His nose hiked into the air, sniffing. His tail thumped hard on the ground before he launched across the kitchen, nails clipping fast. Food rushed into a red plastic dog bowl. "You and I are going to have to eat something. We've got to keep up our strength if we're going to keep up with Oscar."

"Is he even chewing?"

"Nah. I think he's inhaling it whole. Hope it all goes down all right without getting clogged. Do you know the Heimlich for dogs?"

"I do. The bowl's already empty. Incredible."

"Oscar's got skills. Not necessarily good ones." Liam rolled up the bag and hid it in the pantry, making sure the door was securely closed. "Maybe it would be good to get him out of the house. Say, go for a ride?"

"Woof!" Oscar danced at the word, big chocolate eyes sparkling with excitement. He raced to the back door so fast, his hind legs skidded out from under him. "Woof!"

"It's too late to disappoint him now." Liam pulled a ring of keys from his trouser pocket. "C'mon."

"I'm in charge of this training session." Really, she had to hold her ground. She had to keep control because something felt very, very off. Maybe it was the way laugher made his expressive eyes glitter. Or the rolling lilt of his chuckle, inviting and contagious and ending in a deep masculine rumble. Whatever it was, she had to remain unaffected. Remote. Steel.

"I'm not in charge, either," Liam quipped, "so it's only fair. Are you hungry?"

"You mean we're going out to eat?"

"We'll have to since there's nothing here, not anymore." He unhooked the looped leash from a hook on the wall and clipped it to Oscar's collar, not that the dog could stand still. He danced, he hopped, he barked. "It'll be fun."

"Fun? I don't doubt that." Oscar was a laugh a minute. Her feet decided for her. They pulled her inexorably toward the man and his dog. The door opened, Oscar coiled up like a spring. The moment he had enough room he hurled through the door in one mighty leap that took Liam with him. There was a clatter and a boom.

"Are you all right?" She poked her head out the door to see the barbecue grill land on its side on the deck. Did that stop Oscar? Not a chance. Like the lead dog on an Iditarod team, he half dragged, half pulled Liam to a big blue truck.

"Lock up, would you?" Liam's call carried on the wind. With a *bonk,* Oscar's front paw went up on the side of the truck, whining to be let in.

She had her work cut out for her. She twisted the lock button on the inside of the knob, backed onto the deck and closed the door. Sweet Montana breezes ruffled her hair as she turned into the sunshine, feeling light as air. Robins hopped along lush green grass looking for their dinners, and larks twittered from overhead branches as she skirted the downed barbecue and descended the steps toward Liam, who was waiting for her on the other side of the gate.

"I'm glad you signed on for this." He held the door open, his smile wide and as attractive as a toothpaste commercial. He looked far too fine of a man and she felt uncomfortable. Way too close to him.

She could feel the soft fan of his breath on her neck. His hand closed around her elbow to help boost her up into the truck. Definitely too close. Panic licked through her.

"I can't imagine anyone being as understanding with Oscar. Thank you." The deep tones of his voice rumbled smoothly, calm and easygoing. "I tuned in to one of those dog training shows on cable and it scared me a little."

"Sure, because you look scared." She slid onto the seat, trying not to notice the panic galloping through her. He let go, she could breathe, glad to be back in her comfort zone again. "I guess it depends on the kind of relationship you want with your dog."

"Right? That's what I think. I'm not into the militant alpha dog thing. I'm just hoping he won't wreck my house while I'm gone. Is that too much to ask?"

"Who knows?" she quipped. "We'll have to find out."

"If you, the dog trainer, don't have faith, then

who does?" He shut the door for her, framed by the partially open window.

Oscar barked, poked his nose over the seatback and swiped her across the jaw with his tongue. He hopped up and down on the seat like a puppy, watching as his new master circled around the truck, unable to take his doggy gaze from Liam. Those big chocolate eyes reflected a big heart full of love.

That was Oscar's problem, she realized, watching the man climb into his seat, buckle up and plug keys into the ignition. What must it have been like to have been locked up at the shelter? To watch people wander by the kennels and choose other dogs, leaving him behind? What must it have felt like to wonder if anyone would ever want you?

Oscar must have been so relieved and overjoyed when Liam had chosen him, kind and easygoing Liam. It showed in those doggy eyes.

She twisted around in the seat to rub Oscar's head. He bumped up into her hand, panting hard, tongue lolling. Happiness emanated from him with such force, he trembled.

"Are you ready to roll, buddy?" Liam put the truck in gear, watching in the rearview mirror as the dog rocked back onto his haunches, sitting like a good boy. An ear-splitting bark echoed around the passenger compartment in response. "Okay. Then let's go. Brooke, I hope you like Mr. Paco's Tacos."

"Are you kidding? It's a family favorite."

"Good to hear because they give the best dog treats in their drive-thru." He guided the truck down the narrow concrete driveway and onto the tree-lined street. He zipped down the side passenger window halfway so Oscar could stick his nose out and breathe in all those scents as the street went by. "Now where were we?"

"When?"

"Before Oscar interrupted us. I was about to question you some more. Figure out the real Brooke McKaslin. Yes, I remember where I was. Why don't you live closer to your family?"

"Which family, that's the question." She leaned back in her seat, lowering her window, letting the wind play with the ends of her hair. She looked stunning in a simple green summery top and denim shorts, more beautiful than any girl next door he'd ever known. Twice as wholesome, twice as sweet. "I grew up near Miles City but I haven't been back to that part of Montana since I was just out of high school."

She faked a smile, but she probably didn't mean to—she probably thought she pulled it off but he could read the sorrow in her eyes. It was sadness so brief he could have imagined it. She crossed her ankles, sitting prim and as pretty as a picture in a magazine.

"My mom still lives there," she explained. "Marriage to my father embittered her. She grew hard after their divorce. Over the years she's become someone I hardly know. She has her own life. We don't talk much."

"I'm sorry to hear that. Is that why Lil dotes on you?"

"Lil dotes on everyone and I'm grateful for that. She was there for me when my mom wasn't." She bit her bottom lip, perhaps debating whether to stay silent or to say more. He could read between the lines—it wasn't that tough to imagine how painful the rift was between mother and daughter. Again, the pain crossing her face flashed briefly, just one single glimpse before it was gone. "My dad got out of jail not long ago. He was arrested for counterfeiting."

"You don't have the all-American family?"

"Not even close." She shrugged her slender shoulders, as if her troubles were not a big deal in the scale of things. "My older brothers are wonderful. They've stood beside me, and they've never let me down. We were close growing up."

"Yeah? What was that like?" He turned at the end of the street, taking the residential route. Oscar kept entertained dashing between the windows, seeing a squirrel out one window, and racing along the backseat to whine at a cat out the other.

"It wasn't all that interesting. I'll bore you."

"Not even close. I'm riveted. See?"

Her smile could kick-start his heart if he ever found himself in need of a defibrillator. She rolled her eyes. "Before Dad left us, he'd treated Mom pretty badly. We were glad to see him go. He didn't work hard at keeping in contact with us. He was too busy stringing Lil along, promising marriage and I don't know what else. I know he hurt her terribly."

"So you didn't know Lil when you were younger?"

"Not really. We were doing all we could to hold on to the family farm. In the end, we couldn't. Dad had taken a second mortgage out on it when the land values ballooned, right before he took off."

That's all he needed to know about Brooke's dad. She didn't deserve a father like that, one who let her down. "That's rough. It sounds like he didn't treat Lil any better."

"No. I don't know what happened, but she cries about it to this day. By the time he'd gotten married again and the twins were born—"

"Bree and Brandi."

"Yes. He stayed away. That's how I like it."

"How did you all get so close? I've seen the way Lil dotes over you. Colbie champions you. There's a story there, I know it. Don't tell me it's dull. I don't buy it."

"Oh, it's not dull, just best left in the past." There

were so many things she couldn't tell him, places she did not want to speak of. The past—her lost years, finding out exactly how heartless some men could be—it was all best kept safely buried. "There's Mr. Paco's Tacos."

"Saved in the nick of time. Again." He whipped into the parking lot while Oscar poked his nose out the window, gave a deep sniff and barked happily. His tail went *thump, thump, thump* against the back of Brooke's seat.

"Yes, and don't think I won't return the favor." Nothing like a little threat to keep a man in line, she thought as the truck idled at the lit giant menu. "If you can ask questions, then I can ask questions."

"I'm in big trouble now." He tossed a wink.

Handsome. Charming. With killer dimples to match.

Be still my heart, she thought. She prayed. She pleaded. *Don't be affected by him, Brooke. Don't do it.* But could she help it?

No. The world around her faded into nothing, the fears within her faded into silence. And Liam? He took front and center. He was life and color while everything else turned gray.

"Is my head in your way?" He scooted back a little more, as much as his seat would allow. "Can you see all the burrito choices?"

"Not necessary, because I live for Mr. Paco's soft chicken tacos."

"Who doesn't?" The speaker squawked, and a crackling voice asked if they were ready to order. Liam ordered three meals, complete with Mexifried tater tots, sodas and an order of nachos. Oscar barked, eager to talk to Mr. Paco, too.

"Sounds like someone needs a dog treat." The proprietor chuckled warmly. When they pulled up to the window, a big dog-boned–shaped goody waited. Oscar crunched happily on it as Liam tugged out his wallet.

"Don't even think about it," he told her with that smile she couldn't say no to. "This is my treat. You are doing me a favor."

"I haven't done one yet."

"What do you mean? You've already taught me not to leave hamburger out on the counter. That's a start." He handed over a twenty to Mr. Paco, who squinted through the window at her.

"At first I thought you were Colbie, but you're Brooke," he said. "The sister from Seattle. Good to see you again."

"Good to see you." The moment broke like a soap bubble in the air, suddenly and completely. No way to get it back. For a moment she'd forgotten who she was, she'd forgotten her past. Mr. Paco knew. For a moment she'd been able to step away from the woman she'd been. Anxiety beat through her, kicking in her bloodstream right along with the shot of adrenaline.

Please don't say it, Mr. Paco, she silently pleaded. *Don't say what happened nine long years ago.*

"It's good to see you, Brooke." Mr. Paco dug in his till and handed Liam his change. "I've been keeping your sister in prayer."

Oh, Brianna. Relief left her sagging against her seat belt. "Thank you. I know she would be very touched you're lifting her up in prayer. This is a hard time for her."

"She is blessed to have her family nearby. I'll get your sodas. Be right back." Mr. Paco's warm smile telegraphed caring and concern.

"I hear the tough stuff starts tomorrow. In court," Liam clarified. "Recreating the facts of the case. The district attorney is determined to get a conviction."

"He wants justice." She remembered the capable, serious-looking man sitting soldier straight, heading the prosecution. Her family put a lot of faith in him. "For all the victims' sakes, I hope he gets it. We nearly lost Brianna. That's what brought us together. Lil called me with the news they were rushing to catch a plane to Seattle because Bree had been flown to the trauma center there. It was that serious. I didn't even know Lil had my number."

"Sounds like her, taking care of everyone." He stopped to take the bags of food from Mr. Paco, handing them across the console for her to hold.

Warmth penetrated the white paper sacks along with a delicious aroma of seasoned meat, special sauce and salsa. The truck lumbered forward, following the lane to the street.

"It was the first time all of us kids had been gathered together," she confessed.

"I wouldn't have guessed that. Everyone seems close."

"Growing up we didn't have the chance to get to know each other. Then there were all these issues with Dad. After he left the farm, he couldn't settle in a job for long. Then he was arrested and sent to j-jail." She stumbled over the word. That hated word. "We all had our separate lives. But waiting for Bree's condition to improve, praying it would, fearing it wouldn't, forged a bond none of us expected. I got the chance to really know Lil and Colbie. To fall in love with my half sisters. It was an unexpected blessing."

"It seems like the experience of the trial might be doing the same." He spun the wheel, guiding the truck onto the main street, crossing several lanes and heading for the park. Trees speared above buildings a block ahead, guiding the way.

"Definitely." She didn't know how to say what

she felt. How not even the loneliness always dogging her could fade when she was with her family. It came close, but nothing could bridge the stigma she carried around inside her like a secret. Her life had been in shambles for so long, she feared there was no way to repair it.

Something bumped the bags in her hand. Oscar. He leaned over the seat back, trying to dig into the sacks with his nose. Unapologetic, he stopped to squint up at her with pleading eyes.

"There's more dog treats in one of the bags," Liam explained as he wheeled into the park's lot. "Oscar is a fast learner. I'm beginning to think he's smarter than I am."

"That's highly likely," she quipped as she unrolled a sack to peer in. The aroma of deep-fried tater tots wafted upward, making her dizzy with anticipation. Next bag. "He's way smarter than me, too."

Oscar yipped cheerfully, as if he were in perfect agreement.

The laughter in the cab felt wonderful, bright enough to drive away any shadow, except the one haunting her. Fearing what Mr. Paco might have said remained like a whisper within her she could not quiet. Proof you can't escape your past, not entirely. It's always with you. She pulled out a dog treat and handed it over, avoiding Liam's smile.

But the impact of his gaze? That was something

she could feel like a touch against the side of her face. Kind, reassuring, real. He's a good man. But what was hidden beneath the surface? That was an entirely different question.

Chapter Five

"What exactly does this have to do with training the dog?" Liam squinted into the low rays of the sun, gave the Frisbee a flick with his wrist and let it fly.

Across the stretch of green grass, Oscar leaped in anticipation, his gaze trained on the flying red disc hurling his way.

"I'm just observing. Gathering information." Behind him, Brooke looked up from her phone. Her thumbs brushed across the tiny keys, her forehead furrowed in concentration as she bent over the screen. Wisps of dark hair framed her face.

Gorgeous.

Not that he was taking personal interest or anything. Her beauty was simply a plain fact. Thankfully Oscar barked, drawing his attention away from Brooke. But as the dog leaped to catch the Frisbee, Liam's gaze boomeranged right back to her. Amazing. With the wind in her hair, framed by the vivid green grass and leafy trees, she was entirely different from the quiet woman he'd first met sitting alone on her front steps. Different from the serious woman in the courthouse. He liked all sides of Brooke that he'd seen so far, this one the best by far. Just analyzing, he told himself, nothing more.

He cleared his throat. "What info are you in the middle of gathering right now?"

"Doggy day care centers." She folded a strand of hair behind one ear, a graceful gesture, emphasizing the fine curve of her cheek, the line of her jaw and the slender elegance of her fingers. She squinted at her screen. "There's one a mile away from your house. According to their website, they are taking new clients. Wow, they even have a dog gym with an entire day of fun planned activities."

"So you basically think I shouldn't leave Oscar at home alone?"

"Not tomorrow, no. I'm not a miracle worker." Lavender-blue eyes sparkled with amusement. "Oscar is going to take a lot of patience because he is so worried about losing you."

"Oh. I hadn't thought of it that way. Good boy, good dog." He stroked the Lab's head and accepted the Frisbee. It got to him how fast the dog had bonded to him. "You have to wonder about his life before the pound. Whether he had a good home and what it was like for him to be left by the people he loved."

"Yes, but at least they brought him to the pound. That was a great kindness. Some people leave animals alone and defenseless to fend for themselves, which of course they can't. Did the shelter have any information on him?"

"None." The dog danced in place, grinning widely, panting with anticipation. Big doggy eyes stayed glued to the Frisbee waiting for that exciting moment when it went flying. Liam didn't want to disappoint so he gave it a good fling. The Lab transformed into a golden blur, rocketing after it.

"There." She pocketed her cell. "I just texted them. I think Bree and Brandi went to school with the people who run this place. I recognize their names from church."

"Part of me was hoping you were kidding about the doggy day care thing. I feel that's taking the easy way out."

"Oscar's anxiety isn't going to disappear overnight. This will give him a lot of new friends and activities to channel his energy into while you're away for the day."

"Good idea. I wouldn't have thought of it."

"That's why I'm here." Sitting cross-legged in the grass, she made a pretty image. Comfortable, friendly, easy to talk to. She rose from the ground, pure gracefulness. "Oscar has a lot of energy. Does he ever get tired?"

"So far not yet. I've been throwing this thing for almost an hour. Look at him. He hasn't slowed down one bit, but my arm? Ready to fall off." He chuckled. The dog began his return run with the Frisbee clamped neatly between his sharp teeth. "Oscar, do you want to go for a ride?"

At the word, doggy ears pricked. Brown eyes sparkled. The Lab grinned widely around the plastic disk in his mouth, pivoted neatly and bounded toward the distant truck.

"Hey, wait up!" Liam called out, but the dog already loped far ahead. "I didn't think that out real well."

"No? You'll get used to it." Brooke breezed along at his side with the sunshine glinting in her dark locks and caressing the side of her face, polishing her, holding her in the soft golden glow.

There was something ethereal about the moment. The heavenly light, the peaceful evening and the brightness of the park made the evening surreal. The green lawn, blue sky and nodding trees were as vibrant as a scene in a movie. This felt like a monumental moment, defining, one he would not forget.

Brooke whistled. The shrill note sailed on the wind and stopped Oscar in his tracks. The yellow dog swung around on his haunches, ears up, tongue lolling. Brooke laughed. "Wait up, silly boy."

Wasn't she something? The sight of her riveted him. Bronzed in the evening sunlight, carefree and laughing, she was so lovely she made calm settle within him. A deep well of peace he'd never felt before. It was as if his entire soul stilled.

Surely that couldn't be a good sign.

"Come here, boy. Come on!" She patted her knee, calling him in her mellow, warm way. Unable to resist, Oscar bolted across the stretch of the city park. Ears flopping, muscles flexing, paws eating up ground.

"Now it's your turn." She fastened those hyacinth-blue eyes on him, the prettiest color he'd ever seen. She arched one delicate brow, quirked her soft mouth and tilted her head slightly to the left. The effect on him?

Disastrous.

"What's your story?" She squinted. The sun shining into her face kept the intensity of her gaze from hitting him full-force and still he was affected. Panic popped through him because he felt so comfortable with her. He was likely to tell her anything. What had happened to his defenses?

"Which story do you want to know?" A tougher man, one who didn't talk about his feelings, wouldn't be swayed by any woman, even one as gently beautiful as Brooke.

"The one about why adding a dog to your life has been your biggest commitment to date."

She didn't pull any punches, did she? She went straight to what she wanted to know. He fisted his hands, focused on his dog loping all out toward them and noticed a group of people walking along the river trail. Might as well tell her the truth, as tough as that would be. "I was engaged not too long ago."

"Engaged? I didn't know. Colbie and Lil didn't say a thing."

"Probably out of pity. I really got my heart broken." He winced, doing his best not to feel the old hurt, the old bitterness, but they remained steadfast in his heart. "Guess that happens to everyone along the way. Even you?"

"You phrased that as a question and don't think for a moment I'm going to answer it. At least not until you do."

"I was stupid." He may as well confess it.

"It happens, especially when it comes to love. I've done the same thing."

"Yeah?" Curious. "Tell me about it so I don't feel like a chump."

"Oh, no, sorry. I don't go there." She smiled as Oscar leaped at her. "You are trouble, mister."

The dog, not him. Brooke's laughter doubled when Oscar gave her a kiss on the chin. With both paws on her shoulder, the dog gazed lovingly up at her. Captivated.

He understood just how Oscar felt.

"Sidney was a business consultant I met on a flight to London a few years ago." He rescued the Frisbee Oscar had dropped in the grass and the dog bounded over to him. Why he was admitting this, he didn't know. "I used to travel a lot with my job."

"That sounds exciting. Did she travel a lot, too?"

"Yes. That was the beauty of it. We were both busy, on the go. She understood my life because it was hers, too." For a brief moment, the flash of remembered love he'd once felt for the woman transformed him, made him magnificent. He must have loved his Sidney so much. "We talked the entire flight. We just couldn't stop."

"Sounds like you two were a good match."

"I thought so." He took a few steps in the direction of the parking lot and let the Frisbee sail through the air. "I didn't want that plane ride to end. But the wheels touched down and we had to say goodbye. I gave her my cell number, sure I'd never hear from her."

"She called you." Who wouldn't? Brooke could hardly blame the woman. Liam, with the lowering sun slanting behind him like heaven's light, could make even a woman like her want to believe in Prince Charming.

"I knew the moment I heard her voice on the

other end of the line that my life would change. I thought it would be for the better." Self-conscious, he shrugged his impressive shoulders, the ones that would make any woman sigh.

Not that she was sighing.

"Sidney met me for dinner." He stared off in the distance, hardly noticing when Oscar bounded up. The dog had to nudge the Frisbee into his master's hand to draw him back. Liam grabbed the disk and sent it sailing again. "We talked, we laughed, we walked along the Thames. It just felt so right."

"When it wasn't?"

"Exactly." Regret burned dark blue as his gaze narrowed. "I should have known better. Love leads to heartbreak regardless of what books and movies tell us."

"Not every time." She had to believe that was true, that love could flourish somewhere, somehow.

Not for her but for someone. The world would be a very bleak place without everlasting love on it. But then again, maybe it was just wishful thinking.

"How many relationships do you know that have stood the test of time?" Oscar rushed up to him, panting hard, his prize clamped between his teeth. Liam scrubbed the dog's head.

"Oh, tough question." She wrestled with that one herself. "My parents are divorced. My father has divorced twice. The twins' mother has been in and out of marriages."

"My parents are divorced, too. Although they both live in Washington, D.C."

"The lawyers?"

"Both workaholics. Both are Type A."

"Things you inherited?"

"Mostly." He tugged his keys from his pocket, the parking lot nearer now. "Maybe I inherited the bad marriage gene."

"I know the feeling."

"That's why you're still single?"

"One reason." The truth sat on the tip of her tongue, ready to be told. What was she doing? She swallowed hard, holding back the words. What was it about Liam that made her guards weaken? She'd nearly opened up to him. She shook her head. No way did she know him enough to trust him. "It's my opinion men cause destruction and ruin wherever they go."

"Funny, that's my opinion about women." His slow grin made her heart skip a beat.

Good thing her heart wasn't in charge. She was. And she wasn't going to let his stunning smile weaken her defenses any further. Time to shore them up. She hiked her chin and steeled her spine.

"I know that's not fair." Liam winked. "But that's how it feels."

So hard to ignore that wink. She let it bounce

off her, unaffected. She'd gotten as close to him as she was going to. Best to remember she worked for him, she was leaving as soon as the trial was over and the last thing she wanted was a man to complicate things. She had a life again. No way was she going to mess that up.

"Hey, Liam!" A man waved, heading in their direction. He wasn't alone. He held a pretty woman's hand, their wedding bands glinting in the sunshine. A preschooler on a tricycle pedaled in front of them. "Out walking your new dog?"

"Something like that. Roger, Jayne, come meet Oscar."

"Oscar, huh? I couldn't believe that pic you sent me." The man and his family came closer. "How's your living room?"

"It might never be the same again but that's all right. My life needed a little shaking up. And Oscar's a great guy. See?" The friendly dog bounded up sweetly to the little boy, tongue lolling.

"Puppy!" The preschooler shouted with glee and plopped the flat of his hand on the top of the Lab's head. Oscar nuzzled in to swipe kisses across the boy's face. Squeals of joy rang on the wind. Oscar's tail thudded on the ground as he gave the tot another ardent kiss.

"I guess he's good with kids." Jayne patted the dog's head. "He's just a big goofy guy. How fun."

"I can't believe you're out with a pretty lady."

Roger slipped his arm around his wife's shoulders. "Jayne and I had given up hopes you would ever date again."

Date? Did it look as if they were together? Brooke watched a similar shock explode across Liam's face. His mouth opened, he struggled, but no words emerged. Maybe she'd better rescue him.

"This isn't a date. I've got to clear up that misimpression right away," she quipped.

"As if you would want to be with that guy, huh?" Jayne joined in, merry.

"You know it. I'm the dog trainer."

"Aw, mystery solved." Roger chuckled and his gaze fixated on her, narrowing. "You're one of the McKaslin girls."

"Guilty. You must know Lil and Colbie?"

"Sure I do. I interviewed them after Brianna was home from the hospital last year. I covered the Backdoor Burglars case for the *Times*."

"You're a reporter?" That hated word turned sour on her tongue. She took a step back involuntarily. He'd been in the courtroom today. That's why he looked vaguely familiar.

"Yep, I'm a journalist. Believe me, it's tough having Liam for a boss," Roger joked with an obvious mix of good humor and respect.

"Your boss?" The brightness shattered all around her. Surely she hadn't heard that right. She tilted her head and ignored shock quaking through her system. "You work for Liam?"

"Sure, it's a burden I carry well." Roger's jovial tone belied his words. "You're wondering if I got my story filed on time, aren't you, Liam?"

"Hey, that's not my department. You always hit your deadlines."

"He's a bigwig at the paper," Roger explained. "We went through college together. Journalism majors. He's the reason I moved to Montana. His grandfather was kind enough to offer me a job. Here's to old friendships, right, Liam?"

"Hey, I'm not claiming you as my friend." Liam's light quip said differently.

Liam worked at the paper? Shock dulled her senses. She couldn't think but her knees started to quake. How could it be true? She licked her lips and forced out the question. "You're a reporter, too?"

"So they tell me." Liam knelt down to smile at the toddler, still enthralled with Oscar.

Of course, he was a reporter. The pieces clicked into place. That's why he'd been in court. He was covering the story. He knew the reporter who'd approached her by name. That's why he'd asked those questions about her and her family, about Bree and her fiancé.

He'd been getting information out of her. She hadn't even realized it.

Way to go, Brooke. You sure know how to pick 'em. She shook her head, stunned. And here she'd thought he was a good guy.

"I don't write as much as I used to," he went on, as if he hadn't done anything wrong. "I miss it."

"Hey, you can write what you want, since you're second in charge at the paper." Roger winked. "Don't believe his sob story, Brooke. He gets his choice of assignments. And working with his grandfather makes him happy."

"I can't argue with that. My Grandfather Knightly is great. I like hanging with him." Liam rescued the Frisbee Oscar had forgotten in the grass. "Harry is getting big. His birthday is coming up, right? I'm still invited?"

"Of course." Jayne smiled. "How old are you, Harry?"

"Free." He held up three fingers, which Oscar licked happily, tail wagging.

The scene seemed surreal. A terrible ringing clanged in her ears. Her hands turned cold, her knees wobbly. How could she have been so clueless? She swallowed hard, but the knot in her throat wouldn't budge. Why had she let her guard down?

"C'mon, Oscar. Sorry, Jayne, your kid's hair is standing straight up on end. Looks like a Mohawk." Liam grabbed the Lab's collar, tugging him away from the preschooler. The dog's tongue dangled, torn away mid-lick.

"It's a new look for our little guy. He's going punk," Roger joked as the family moved off together. "See you at tomorrow's staff meeting?"

"I'll be there bright and early."

"Nice meeting you, Brooke," Jayne called out, friendly.

"You, too." The words felt torn out of her. She pasted what she hoped was a pleasant smile on her face for the kind woman. Wooden, she took a step, alone with Liam as the little family moved off.

What if she'd opened up to Liam more? What if she'd told him the truth about her past? Look what might have happened. Her family secrets and her past spilled all over his grandfather's newspaper, that's what. She shook her head, stumbling after the man and his dog. She couldn't believe how close she'd come to making another mistake.

Be careful who you trust. Hadn't she learned that lesson well enough the first time? Liam strode a few steps ahead of her with his dog, as easygoing and amiable as he'd always been.

"How long have you been a reporter?" Her hands fisted. She kept her head down, holding back her anger, trying to corral her hurt. "Since college?"

"Yeah. Once I graduated, my grandfather wanted me to help him run his paper but I wasn't ready. I headed off to New York. Started as a stringer for the *New York Times* and worked my way up." He shrugged, modest, not elaborating. Most men she knew didn't hesitate to show a little ego. "Like I said, my folks hoped I would take after them, but reporting was in my blood. When I landed a job at a cable news network, I couldn't believe it."

"So that explains why you said you traveled a lot." The pieces finally fit. She'd been interested in the broken romance part of his story instead of asking the right questions, like what he did for a living. "I don't watch the news a lot, but it sounds fascinating. You were a foreign correspondent?"

"I traveled all over the globe. It was exciting." He hit the remote on his key chain. His truck locks popped open and the dog loped ahead, overjoyed by the prospect of another ride. Liam didn't even seem to realize she was upset. Maybe he hadn't tried to trick her on purpose, but that certainly didn't change the facts.

She'd trusted him more than she should have. Well, not anymore. This was about the dog, she reminded herself. And don't forget her pocketbook. She could use the money. Oscar needed help. It didn't have to be any more complicated or personal than that.

"Are you okay?" He broke the brief silence. "You seem a little quiet."

"I'm fine." Wiser, but fine. "I'm thinking we should make a few stops on the way back. The hardware store. The pet store."

"My thoughts exactly. We're on the same wavelength, you and me." He winked, charming, looking like everything good and trustworthy in the world. He strode through the sun with the wind tousling his hair and the happy dog at his side.

But was she charmed? Not a chance. Not again. She shrugged, not sure what to say. It was best to keep her distance from this moment on.

Chapter Six

"It's getting late." Brooke's voice broke the silence between them that had settled into the house once they'd returned. He wanted to attribute it to the long day and the fact they had a daunting task ahead of them, but he wasn't sure. She'd been quiet before they left the park.

After they met Roger and his wife.

He glanced at the mantel clock, put down the instruction sheet and stood, his back protesting. "It's nearly nine. We got a lot done in the past two hours. You were phenomenal."

"Not so much. The cleanup looked worse than it really was." She didn't meet his gaze as she stowed the broom in the entry closet. "Poor Oscar. He must have been so upset worrying you wouldn't come back."

"He's worn himself out. Look." The dog snoozed on his bed in the corner, legs sticking straight out, snoring like a truck downshifting on the freeway. "The more I think about that day care idea, the more I like it."

"We'll try to work on his anxiety again next time. If you want." All business, she tugged the bag of dog treats from her purse and left them on the coffee table. Eyes down, polite, distant.

"Sounds good. You made a real difference today. Thanks. Plus, Oscar has taken a liking to you."

"I'm not falling for that. Oscar adores everyone." A hint of a smile touched her lips but she still didn't look up. Keys in hand, she faced the door. "Looks like you got the kennel figured out?"

"Yep, it's all in one piece. I have faults but I'm great at following directions." Another quip, but she didn't smile. She didn't banter back. She just slipped her purse strap higher on her shoulder. Her attention arrowed to the door, once again like the serious woman he'd first spotted in Lil's yard.

He remembered Tasha Brown rushing her in the corridor. He didn't know what that was about, but it probably had something to do with when Brianna was in the hospital over in Seattle. Brooke lived in Seattle. He had no idea what all had gone on there because he'd been out of the country. But it struck him now that she'd asked a few questions about his job after meeting Roger.

"I'll walk you out." Tension tugged tight in his chest, growing worse with every step. A war waged inside him—to keep his distance versus the unexplainable hold she had on him. He cared about her. He couldn't help it. Truth was, she was a hazard to him. Her gentleness, her quirky humor and now the quiet pull of her spirit got to him.

Even when he'd sworn no woman ever would.

The brass doorknob felt cool against his palm as he gave it a twist. Lukewarm night air washed over him as he held the door open for her. When she whispered past, a gust of wind carried her vanilla scent. A few strands of her long hair brushed against his jaw.

Caring rolled through him with such force he had to brace his feet and steel his spine not to give in to it. A hazard? The woman was a live minefield. He tripped down the steps after her, reeling. A smart man would say good-night and retreat into the house while he could, but was he a smart man?

Well, that had always been in debate. He trailed after her down the shadowed walkway, unable to take his focus away from the lithe silhouette she made.

"You didn't know I was a reporter, did you?" His question made her turn around in the darkest part of the yard. He couldn't see her but he didn't need to. He felt her gaze on him and heard the intake of her gasp.

"No, I didn't. No one thought to inform me. Even you." No accusation in her soft tone. Steady, solid, unemotional, as if she'd already retreated too far to come back.

Maybe he should be glad for that. Maybe he should be shouting out a cheer, jumping up and down in relief because the bid to keep her from affecting him just got easier. But he couldn't let it go. She might not admit it and she refused to show it, but she was hurting.

He hated that.

"I thought you knew. It's a lame excuse, I know. I shouldn't have assumed. I should have tattooed it on my forehead or something." That quip garnered a better reaction. He could feel her smile and the knot of tension wedged in his chest began to ease. "Your family knows what I do for a living. It's not a secret."

"No, I get it. I understand." So she said, but the distance between them didn't change. Her tone didn't warm. Her guards didn't go down. "I see what happened."

"You don't have to worry about Roger. He's mostly harmless. He wouldn't have grilled you like Tasha tried to do."

"It's not Roger I'm worried about." She exhaled, a sigh of frustration. "You basically interviewed me without my knowledge or permission."

"Interviewed you? When?"

"All those questions about Bree."

Realization hit him like a hammer. The blow

struck hard, reverberating through him down to his bone marrow. What an idiot he'd been, a complete and utter dummy. No wonder she was upset. He risked taking a step closer. "I never intended to print anything you've told me off the record. That's the way I am. Ask Lil. Ask Colbie. They know."

"I guess we'll see in tomorrow's paper." Her dark silhouette moved slightly, her chin going up. She didn't believe him.

He drew himself up to his full height but he didn't feel tall enough, good enough, not any longer. Not in Brooke's eyes. She was wrong, but he knew what she saw, what this looked like. He disliked it, he really did, because he'd hurt her. At least, she thought he had. "I wasn't using you. I wasn't on the job. Nothing that happens between you and me off the record or with any member of your family will wind up in an article of mine. My word of honor."

"I've heard that phrase before."

"You haven't heard it from me. All I'm asking for is a chance. Wait and see what kind of man I am before you quit on Oscar."

"I didn't say anything about quitting on Oscar." The confession scraped from her, grating against her throat.

"I know, but it's something I fear." A hint of humor, always that humor lightening the moment. She could see the shadow of a day's growth along his square jaw and smell the night air on his shirt. He crossed his arms over his chest, a powerful pose, a handsome one. But did it affect her?

Not even close. Her guards were up and they would stay that way. She gave a little prayer of thanks as Liam followed her down the last of the walkway. Streetlamps rained a puddle of light over the pickup, guiding her, leading her away.

"Thanks for everything you've done. You went beyond the call of duty, Brooke." He ambled over to opened the pickup's door. Sincerity defined him. Tall, solid, real. "You saved us."

"Hardly. I just helped a little, that's all." She should hop onto the seat, start the engine and drive away, but something held her back. It was concern for the dog—yes, that's what it had to be. "I hope Oscar likes day care."

"Me, too. I didn't know what I was thinking just picking up a dog with no forethought or preparation. I don't know the first thing about owning a dog."

"I can see how it happened. Who would think twice when it comes to Oscar? Of course you wanted him." She smiled, beauty in the night. "Goodbye."

"Wait. What do I owe you?" He reached for his wallet, but she waved him away.

"We can decide that later. After we see how successful I am. You may change your mind about me and want a real professional." She shook her head, scattering tendrils of dark, silken hair. Those gossamer strands brushed against the curve of her cheek and the line of her jaw the way his hand itched to.

He didn't reach out as much as he wanted to. Brooke had put distance between them and he wasn't going to cross it. Distance was a good idea. So good, he took a step back, barricading his feelings with all his might.

No way was he getting involved again and if he did, it wouldn't be with a woman who was as reserved as Brooke. After talking with her half the evening, she remained a great big mystery. She kept a part of herself hidden away just like Sidney did. Besides, he liked Brooke far too much for safety. That was the best reason to pull back.

"Drive safely. Maybe I'll see you tomorrow." He eased onto the sidewalk while the engine started. Kept to the shadows. He could be a mystery, too.

Brooke lifted her hand in a dainty little wave, giving him nothing more, not even a smile, before the truck pulled away.

He watched the taillights grow smaller in the darkness until with a faint red flicker they faded away.

The crescent moon peeked over the trees rimming the trailer park. Brooke climbed out of the borrowed pickup and into the faint moonlight. Lights shone from neighbors' windows but no one else was out. Not a single car motored by. No dogs barked. No cats prowled the shadows. Gripping her bag, she headed up the stairs, breathing in the sweet Montana air redolent with the scents of lilacs and early budding roses. Upset clung to her no matter how hard she tried to stop it. *Just brush it off, Brooke.* She paused on the porch to take a cleansing breath. It had been a close call tonight. Why had she let her guard down? She had no clue why Liam affected her that way.

"Brooke, there you are! I thought I heard the truck." The door swung open before she could reach it. Brandi held a bowl of ice cream in one hand, gripping the doorknob with the other. She looked adorable as always dressed in a Montana State University T-shirt and shorts with her light blond hair tied back in a long swooping ponytail. "You're just in time. We're having zero-calorie dessert."

"There's a brand of ice cream with no calories?"

"Sure. In my imagination." Brandi laughed.

"In mine, too," Bree called with an identical cheer from the kitchen. She held a bowl in one hand and a freshly loaded spoon with another. "Come in and have some no-cal mint chocolate chip."

"I'm not sure I'm that imaginative. I see calories," she teased. "Lots and lots of calories."

"Hey, I'm in denial over here," Colbie called from the kitchen. "Don't mess with my denial!"

"Sorry. My bad."

"Don't just stand out there, dear, come tell us all about it." Lil gestured from her chair with the hand that wasn't holding an enormous bowl of ice cream. "Did you have fun tonight?"

"Oscar was a hoot." She closed the front door behind her and plopped her purse onto the small entry table. "I found him a spot at the Dillards' day care."

"Good choice. They're such nice people." Colbie scooped ice cream from the container and into a bowl. "I'm sure he'll be happy there."

"That should keep him out of trouble, but that's not what we all wanted to know." Brandi waggled her brows as she dug into her ice cream. "So, how did things go with Liam?"

"Yes, tell us all about Liam." Lil hit Pause on the remote, freezing the legal drama on the screen mid-cross-examination. "He's such a handsome man and a real gentleman. You two seem to get along."

"Looks can be deceiving. He's a reporter. You guys could have told me what I was walking into."

"Guess I didn't think of it." Bree ambled out of the kitchen and gave her spoon a lick. "He asked me for an interview and I'm giving him one right after my testimony."

"He already got an unofficial one from me." She hated to be the one to break their illusions about Liam, but she had to be honest. "He asked me a lot of questions, which I answered without knowing his agenda. Questions about you, Bree."

"I'm sure it's nothing. He won't use what you told him. Honestly. Trust me. He knows if he wants a quote, he can call." She slipped into an overstuffed chair facing the TV. "Hey, did you get supper? We can warm up leftovers if you're hungry." That was Brianna, as sweet as could be. She sat next to her twin, totally unconcerned. Clearly she didn't understand the situation.

"I ate, thanks. I'm sorry, I should have wondered why he was asking all those questions. He just seemed like a concerned friend of the family."

"That's because he is. We've known Liam for a long time." Colbie opened the cabinet in search of another bowl. "What kind of ice cream do you want? Mint chocolate chip, strawberry shortcake or triple fudge?"

"The chocolatey one." Did Colbie really have to ask?

"Liam's not like some of those reporters who hounded us when Bree was in the hospital," Brandi explained.

"Or like the ones who descended after your arrest," Bree finished. The twins nodded together, blond heads bobbing, heart-shaped faces dimpling, two peas in a pod.

Liam had said he wouldn't use what she'd told him. But what he actually *did* was a different matter. And the mention of her arrest? That was just the ultimate reminder why she should never trust another man again. Darren had betrayed her trust in the worst possible way.

"Is this enough or do you want another scoop?" Colbie held up a bowl heaping with ice cream.

"Give her another scoop," Brandi called from the couch, pushing a stray strand of light blond hair from her eyes. "We have to fatten her up while we can…"

"…and spoil her as long as she's here." Bree finished her twin's thought with a cute grin. "Then maybe we can change her mind about going back to Seattle."

"I guess at this point it depends on how my job hunt pans out. Colbie, that's a whole lot of ice cream."

"No calories, remember? So it doesn't matter." Colbie plunged a spoon into the mountain of chocolate and handed over the bowl. "I'm praying hard. Maybe, just maybe, you can stay. Training Liam's dog is a start, right?"

Brooke did her best not to imagine Liam laughing in the sunshine tossing a Frisbee. She tried not to remember how kindly he treated his dog. Her throat tightened and she felt at a loss. "It's just one very temporary job."

"But it could turn into another. You know how word of mouth works." Colbie grabbed her by the arm and forcefully steered them both toward the living room. "You do one good job, people talk, and next thing you know you have more work than you can handle. Maybe you will become the premier dog trainer in Bozeman."

"That's quite an imagination you have." Her sisters. Who wouldn't love 'em? She slipped onto the edge of the couch. "Premier dog trainer? I can't see it."

"Maybe it's time to start dreaming again, Brooke." Lil worked her spoon in her ice cream. "You ought to think about what you want to do next with your life."

"Maybe." Agreeing was easier than admitting she didn't know how to get her dreams back. She'd been out of jail nineteen months, and half of that time she'd spent struggling to find the basics—shelter, food, work, purpose.

"You always wanted to be a vet assistant." Brandi paused over a spoon piled high with mint chocolate chip. Her forehead crinkled adorably. "I could check around. Maybe MSU has a program or something. We could be college buddies, you, me and Bree."

"But aren't you two almost finished?" The ice

cream really did smell good and fudgy. Her mouth watered traitorously. She stared at the bowl, debating. As much as she wanted to she couldn't deny the calories away. Colbie had dished up enough for three people, but did that stop her from digging into it?

No way.

"We're going to look into it anyway. End of argument." Bree licked at her spoonful of ice cream.

"Excellent. It's a great plan." Colbie settled into the middle couch cushion with a bounce. "We want you to stay, Brooke, and it's a great deal for you. We know you love animals, so it's the perfect profession for you. You could meet lots of dashing college students. When you graduate there's always handsome pet owners and hunky veterinarians. I say it's a win-win."

"And a guy is so not what I need." She rolled her eyes, shook her head and thought of Liam. Why did she think of Liam? Probably because of the words *handsome* and *hunky*. A natural combination that defined the man.

Get him out of your head, Brooke. She popped a spoonful of chocolate into her mouth, richly delicious and cold enough to freeze the roof of her mouth. Ouch.

"Speaking of hunky and handsome." Bree leaned forward, turning the intensity of her lavender-blue eyes on Colbie. "Did you notice the D.A.?"

"The district attorney?" Colbie asked offhand, as if she hadn't a clue who Bree was talking about. "I guess. Was he the tall one?"

"Yes, he was the tall one." Bree rolled her eyes, not believing Colbie for a second.

"Tall and handsome. Those shoulders." Brandi picked up where her twin left off. "We caught you looking at him."

"Sure, I had to, since he was sitting between me and the witness box." Colbie shrugged indifferently and a silken lock of dark hair tumbled over her slender shoulder. Wistfulness glinted in her expressive eyes for a brief moment.

Interesting. Brooke wondered if she was the only one who noticed it before Colbie plunged her spoon into her bowl, mashing up her scoops of fudge ice cream.

"That district attorney would make a better door than a window," she said as if she didn't care about him at all. "I couldn't see a thing with him blocking the way. Bree, any chance your fiancé has a friend you can fix Brandi up with? One with nice shoulders. Apparently that's important to her."

"Integrity is important to me," Brandi spoke up, swinging her spoon in the air for emphasis. "Steadfastness, loyalty, honesty, the list goes on and on. Notice I'm not dating anyone? That's why. No one can live up to my standards."

"I found a Prince Charming." Love polished

Bree, making her more lovely than ever. "There's no reason you can't find one, too."

"I don't know. There aren't many fairy tales out there ready to come true." Brandi set her chin, not ready to believe. "I'm glad you found one, but I'm grateful to be right here with all of you, my sisters. And Lil."

"I'm thankful, too, dear." Emotion glinted in the older woman's eyes as she grabbed the remote. The screen came to life, sound filled the room as they all leaned back into the cushions to watch the drama unfold.

It was good to be part of a family again.

Chapter Seven

By the time he raced into the morning courtroom, Brooke had already arrived. She was seated near the front with her family behind the D.A.'s table, which was empty. Folks milled about, conversations buzzed and Roger left his side to get their seats. They'd departed the staff meeting early, leaving his grandfather happily in charge, but the satisfaction from working alongside Pop remained. Liam was glad he'd let the Lord guide his steps back home to Bozeman.

What he wasn't glad for was the way his gaze arrowed to Brooke against his will. He really needed an eye exam or something. Maybe a brain scan to solve the mystery of why he couldn't look away from her. Something really had to be wrong with him. And his feet because they took him straight to her.

She looked amazing this morning in slim-cut

slacks, a summery-blue top and matching cardigan. Her hair fell in a long sleek curtain framing her heart-shaped face. When her violet-blue gaze met his, the impact rocked him back a few steps.

Wary. That's what he read in her eyes.

Good, because he was wary, too.

"Good morning, McKaslins." His voice sounded strained and gruff, so he cleared it.

"Liam!" Lil twisted in her wheelchair, adorable as always with her dark cap of hair and apple cheeks. "How good to see you. How is your grandfather?"

"The same. Tough. Stubborn. A rascal."

"And you're a chip off the old block." When she smiled, Lil was a handsome woman. He always kept her in prayer, trapped in that wheelchair. The strain of the trial looked to be getting to her. Smudges bruised the skin beneath her eyes and she looked pale. Pale, but resolute. Nothing could dim her determined smile as she leaned closer. "I hear Brooke found a solution for your dog."

"A good one. Last time I saw Oscar, he was leaping around in the doggy gym chasing a big red ball. He's making all kinds of new friends." His gaze slinked back to Brooke. He wasn't powerful enough to stop it. But was Brooke watching him? No. She was focused squarely on Lil. Probably a good thing and he relaxed a bit. "So far no one from the day care has called to say Oscar's in trouble, so I'm staying cautiously optimistic."

"I hope he has a lot of fun," Colbie broke in. "You should bring him over next time you're in the neighborhood. I'd love to meet him."

"I'll be swinging by tonight." Why he felt obligated to offer that information, he couldn't say. He couldn't seem to stop himself. "I owe Gram a ham."

"Yes, Madge told me all about it." Lil chuckled. "Said she was going to dog sit for you and intended to keep a close eye on him. He's not allowed in the kitchen ever again."

"That settles it," Bree spoke up. "We're having supper at Lil's again tonight. I want to meet Oscar. I love dogs."

"Me, too." Brandi leaned over the bench. "We are way too busy these days for a pet, so we'll have to borrow him."

"If you need a dog sitter—" Bree offered.

"—you know who to call," Brandi finished.

"You two do not know what you're getting into," he warned them, aware of every breathe Brooke took, aware of how deliberately she kept her head turned toward her sisters and not him.

Good. That's just the way he wanted it. He had to ignore the tightness gathering in his chest. She simply had that effect on him—he would get used to it.

"How are you doing, Brianna?" He asked as a family friend, not a reporter. "Are you holding up okay?"

"I'm good. The tough part starts today." Bree swallowed hard. She tightened her grip on her fiancé's hand. Max Decker, a detective with the city, was a good guy. One of the best. They exchanged greetings.

It was easy to read the worry on the man's face and his concern for his Brianna. Infinite devotion shone in those dark eyes. Sometimes love worked out. It was good to see.

"I've got Max, and I've got family around me." Strength showed beneath as Bree lifted her chin. "This will be good in the end. I get to face it and when the trial is over, I'm praying for justice and closure. After all, I wasn't the one hurt the most that awful night."

She glanced a few rows over where Juanita's family was settling in. They had lost a daughter during the robbery. He ached for them. "I'm keeping you all in prayer. You need something, anything, let me know, okay?"

"Thanks, Liam." Bree's quiet smile telegraphed caring and something else. She cast her gaze across the others to Brooke. Brooke, trying hard to avoid him, bit her bottom lip adorably.

His chest cinched tighter. He ignored that, too. "I'd better get settled. The D.A. just walked in."

"Thanks for coming down, Liam," Colbie spoke up with a grateful smile. "Your support means a lot."

"Hey, you've been a friend and a good neighbor to Gram for a long time. Don't forget. I mean it. If I can do something, you call. Got it?" He backed up the aisle, glancing over his shoulder to make sure he didn't ram into anyone.

"Don't worry, we have your number." Lil winked.

"Good. Use it." He seemed to mean it. Caring deepened the summer-dawn blue of his eyes and for a second his gaze held with Brooke's. The shock rolled through her like thunder, rattling her bones before he whipped around, leaving her pulse thumping in her ears.

"He's a gem," Lil trilled as she watched him stride down the aisle. "I just love him. He's so good to his grandmother, always visiting. He gave up a lot to help out when his paternal grandfather got that diagnosis."

"What diagnosis?" The question popped out. She didn't mean to ask. She wasn't interested; she wasn't fishing for information about Liam and his life.

"Cancer. They found it early and Ed's doing well. Liam gave up a big-time job to run the paper while his grandfather was in treatment. Now he's staying on so Ed only has to work part-time. Doesn't that say a lot about the boy?" Lil's hand patted Brooke's. "I—"

"Excuse me." A deep voice belonging to the tall, striking district attorney broke in. Austin Quinn could have been a TV star with his rugged good looks, polished presentation, perfect dark suit and striped tie. But did Brooke's heart skip a beat?

No. Not even a stumble. Regardless of how hard she tried, she couldn't ignore Liam. He'd stopped to chat with Juanita's family. She had a perfect view of him out of the corner of her eye. Not that she was intentionally looking; he was naturally in her field of vision. Caring warmed his handsome features, softened his powerful masculine stance and roped her in. He clearly was just a friend checking in and not doing his reporter thing.

He'd been true to his word. She'd read Lil's morning paper front to back. There hadn't been a single article by Liam Knightly. Roger's recap of the trial had been a facts-based and thoughtful account of the opening day, proving the kind of newspaper Liam and his grandfather ran. Liam had been true to his word.

Not that she was going to let that soften her.

"I'll fight hard, I promise you." The district attorney's molasses-rich voice caught her attention. It took all her strength to turn toward him and away from Liam.

Something kept trying to pull her back, something she did her best to resist as her brothers, arriving from their farm an hour out of town, hurried down the aisle just in time for court to begin.

Brooke shifted on the hard bench as the morning session progressed, fighting her own memories. Trying to stay in the present moment and not to remember sitting next to her defense attorney with the jury's eyes on her. Doing her best not to remember the time when her life hung in the balance.

The observers in the courtroom seemed to take a collective breath as the young college-age woman tapped her way to the witness box, her high heels striking the tile like hammer blows in the silence.

"How are you doing?" Colbie leaned in to whisper. "This isn't reminding you of your court date?"

"A little, but I'll be okay." Her chin went up, buoyed by her determination. The past couldn't get to her. It couldn't defeat her. She refused to be pulled back into those memories of defeat and hopelessness.

"*If I take the wings of the morning, and dwell in the uttermost parts of the sea, even there Your hand shall lead me, and Your right hand shall hold me.* It was my morning devotional verse. You're not alone." Colbie paused while the woman on the stand raised her right hand. "I can see how hard this is for you. You're completely pale."

"You should be thinking about Bree. I can't imagine how hard this has to be for her." Her whisper wobbled, nearly betraying her. "Don't worry about me, okay?"

"I can't help it."

The district attorney pushed out of his chair, approaching the witness in a slow, measured stride. His buttery baritone broke the tense silence. Overhead the buzz of fluorescent lights, the echoed rustles from the audience and the solemn moment threatened to dig deep and hook those memories she fought to suppress.

A little help, Lord, please. She leaned on Him in prayer, feeling uncomfortable. Maybe she shouldn't be leaning on anyone. She'd made the decisions that had changed her life, not God.

"It was just a few minutes before seven." The hostess who'd been on shift the night of the robbery stopped to draw in a shaky breath. She looked small and vulnerable on the stand.

Brooke knew how that felt.

"I was just about to seat a seven o'clock reservation when the front doors burst open so hard, they crashed into the doorstops. Everyone jumped. People waiting began screaming," the hostess said.

Brianna had been in that restaurant. Brooke covered her face with her hands, remembering her half sister ashen and motionless in ICU, the sister she'd barely known at the time.

"I'll never forget the way the light gleamed off the rifle barrel," the hostess continued. Her voice cracked. "I saw the gun before I saw anything else. My mind screeched to a stop. One moment everything was fine, peaceful and my biggest worry was figuring out how to accommodate a large last-minute group and the next thing I hear is gunfire."

That's how it happens, Brooke thought. One moment everything was normal, but the next? Wham. Everything changed. Brianna had been loading her tray in the kitchen and the next moment she'd been critically shot.

That's what had happened in her life, too. One moment she'd been sitting in her car, hand on the steering wheel, engine idling at the border into Canada and the next moment a search dog barked. The border patrol ordered her out of her car and she'd watched in horror as they searched her trunk to find several bricks of heroin in a brown grocery bag tucked next to the spare tire. She could still feel the jerk rocketing up her arm as rough hands spun her around. Cold metal handcuffs clamped around her wrists.

You're not going to remember, right, Brooke? She tried to will down the memory. It was stubborn. Colbie's hand covered hers and squeezed in reassurance. Tears burned behind her eyes as she squeezed back, grateful for the comfort and the strength. The past faded away, leaving her solidly in the present surrounded by family members she loved.

Life was definitely getting better. She would focus on that. She took a steadying breath, relaxed against the back of the seat and ignored the tingle on the nape of her neck. No way was she going to turn around because she knew it was Liam. The tug of her heart, the pull against her soul and the awareness of him did not relent.

But she was stronger. She straightened her spine, stared straight ahead and forced herself to forget he was in the room.

After a grim day of testimony, Oscar's exuberant cheer felt uplifting. With the windows rolled down they drove across town while the Lab ran back and forth from window to window, sniffing and panting. Every now and then he'd poke his nose over the back of the seat to swipe his tongue across Liam's ear or try to poke into the grocery bag on the front passenger seat.

"Sorry, buddy. Not going to happen." As he turned right into the neighborhood, he reached over to nudge the sack out of the lab's reach. "If Gram doesn't get this ham, she might revoke dog sitting privileges. Is that what you want?"

With a quirk of his doggy brows, Oscar panted happily. Perhaps the only word he'd understood was *ham*.

"You resist the ham, got it? I know it's tough, but try. Hanging with Gram is a lot better than the kennel at home. I fixed it up real nice, but something tells me you're not much of a loner." He chuckled as Oscar panted in agreement. What a great idea it had been to get a dog. The best idea he'd ever had.

"There you are." Gram straightened from her flowerbeds, clapping dirt from her snazzy pink gardening gloves. She peered at him from beneath her straw hat's brim. "I heard from your mother not long ago. She said to call her. It was news to her you'd gotten a dog."

"I've been busy." He grabbed the ham before he climbed out of the truck. He was learning. He opened Oscar's door. "I'll call her over the weekend. Look what I have for you."

"It's about time. Don't think I'm up to forgiving that dog of yours." A hint of a grin curved her disapproving mouth, ruining the pretense. "How about it, dog? Are you gonna help yourself to my ham again?"

Oscar hit the ground on all fours, barking happily. His nose worked as he sniffed the air, harboring ham hopes as his tail zinged back and forth.

"Just like I thought. That one's not to be trusted." Gram took charge of the ham, feigning disgruntlement. "I see you didn't take my advice and return him."

"I've sort of gotten attached."

"That's the problem with a dog. They can capture your heart pretty quick. Not mine, mind you, but some people's." Gram sounded tough but she couldn't fool him. "I hope he's not being too much trouble."

"No, I'm the problem. I should have put in more research before I got him." He was to blame. Brooke was right about that. Thinking of her made his chest tighten. "You know me. I'm all sorts of trouble."

"Yes, you are, young man. Don't know how I've managed to put up with you all these years." Amusement shone beneath her gruff tone. "Don't know quite why."

"Maybe the free newspaper subscription helps?" He held open the door for her.

"Yep, a free morning paper. That's the real reason I put up with you." Amused, Gram shuffled into the kitchen, presumably to put the ham safely in the refrigerator where Oscar couldn't get it. "How did the trial go today? I was fixing supper when Lil and the girls came home so I didn't get a chance to head outside and talk with 'em."

"The D.A. has a tight case. I think it's going to get interesting, but it's got to be hard for the families involved." He thought of Brooke again. She'd come to town for her sister's sake and she would be leaving when the trial was done.

Another reason not to keep his guard up.

"What a terrible thing those robbers did. I'm good friends with young Juanita's grandmother." Although the wall divided them, he didn't have to see her face to measure her sadness for her friend. It knelled in her voice like a funeral bell. "Such a loss. And poor Brianna. We came close to losing her, too."

"I know." With the windows open to let in the pleasant May breeze, noise came in, too. The putter of a motorcycle driving by, the slam of someone's screen door, the murmur of conversation. A woman's shriek rolled in on the breeze, followed by a peal of laughter he would recognize anywhere.

Brooke. His heart kicked into overdrive. He pulled back the sheers trying to look out before realizing the fence blocked most of the view of Lil's yard.

Oscar's ears pricked. He barked loud and zealously. Chocolate-brown eyes met Liam's, as if to ask, "Where is she? Where is she?"

Gram paraded into the living room. "I guess you may as well get on your way. Leave the leash by the door. Tell me you've got that monster trained."

"If I did, I would be lying. But he's better than he was on Sunday." He brushed a kiss on his grandmother's cheek, patted Oscar on the head and veered toward the door. "You be good while I'm gone, okay? I won't be long."

Oscar's ears pricked, his head tilted as if he was thinking "huh?"

The minute the door closed shut behind him, a dog's heartbroken yowl shattered the peaceful evening.

"That's Oscar," a familiar voice commented on the other side of the fence as a screen door slapped shut. Brooke. He could imagine her standing on Lil's porch. "I would recognize that howl anywhere."

"It's worse than that emergency broadcast signal," someone answered—Colbie, he guessed. "I'm not sure I've heard anything as annoying. It's amazing."

Amazing. That was the word as he poked his head around the fence post where Gram's lilacs ended and Lil's roses began. He lost his breath at the sight of Brooke in denim shorts, a turquoise top and bare feet, her hair caught up in pigtails.

She was a seriously beautiful woman and he was seriously not going to notice.

"Liam." Colbie spoke first, breaking into her open smile as she lowered what looked like a giant squirt gun. "Is Oscar all right? I mean, what's up with that crying?"

"Separation anxiety, or so I'm told." His stubborn gaze remained glued to Brooke. "Gram said she'd watch him. It's my volunteer night and I didn't want him to get lonely at home."

"Or deafen your neighbors." Colbie laughed, tapping down the steps, her old pair of sneakers squeaking. "It totally slipped my mind that you spend a lot of time at the community youth center. Do you know who else does a lot of volunteer work?"

He knew the answer before she continued. He braced for it.

"Brooke." Colbie landed on the walkway, her free hand firmly grasped around her older half sister's wrist, dragging her into the grass. "I think you should invite her along. I'm on this campaign to get her to move here. You could help me convince her. How about it?"

"Colbie, I'm sure that's the last thing Liam wants to do. To be saddled with me for two evenings in a row." Brooke rolled her eyes—cute—and stared at the ground. Perhaps a little embarrassed.

So was he. He liked Brooke, but distance remained between them. It was a good idea.

"You're always saying how the center needs more volunteers." Colbie gave her neon-blue plastic rifle a hitch, like she was getting ready for a military campaign. "Here's your chance. If Brooke finds a great place to volunteer, then it will be impossible for her to leave."

"See? This is why I miss Seattle." Brooke swiped damp bangs from her forehead—obviously she'd taken a hit from Colbie's rifle. "No nosy, pushy sisters there."

"I know you miss me." Colbie laughed, tilted her head. "Ooh, listen. The dog's quieted down. Well, I'm going to go. I'm on the hunt for the twins. Liam, did I mention Brooke is practically a volleyball champion?"

"I'm not a champion. Honestly." She shook her head. Unbelievable. Could her sister be any more obvious? "I'm fair to middling, that's all. I take it the youth center has something to do with volleyball?"

"Yep, a game twice a week. You must be good if Colbie says so." He strode toward her, interested now. "If you're looking for a good cause, then talk your sisters into bringing you down to the center. It's fun, you'll be helping out a great group of kids and we need women volunteers. There are a lot of girls in need of solid role models."

"I'm no role model." She hoped he didn't see her as one because that only meant he didn't see her at all.

"That's just your opinion." Kind, that almost blinding smile as he came close enough for her to see the five o'clock shadow hugging his square jaw. "You said you like to make a difference. I'm just saying. Colbie and the twins know where the center is. Just think about it, okay?"

No. That's what she should say, but what came out? "Okay."

"Good news for the center." He jingled his keys, backing away. "Maybe I'll see you there."

How did the man become more irresistible every time she saw him? Dressed in a gray T-shirt, athletic shorts and shoes, he could have walked off the pages of a sports magazine, hunky and buff with a wholesome boy-next-door glow.

She was iron. Unmovable. Unalterable. Indestructible. She was not going to soften her stance toward the guy.

"Yes, you will see her there. I'll make sure of it!" Colbie called, but her words were cut short with a shriek as the twins leaped from behind a lilac bush and ambushed her with a water balloon.

Chapter Eight

"I miss Seattle," Brooke commented dryly from the backseat of Colbie's SUV. "Quiet, peaceful, solitary Seattle."

"Ha-ha. We're so not fooled." Brandi squished in next to her and gave her a shoulder bump. "Admit it. You love us."

"I'll admit no such thing." She had to bite her bottom lip to keep from laughing. "This is practically kidnapping."

"True." Unrepentant Colbie turned into a crowded parking lot. "If I didn't have my water rifle, I'm not sure we could have convinced you to get in the car."

"We could have always used my water balloons," Bree pointed out, stifling laughter. "Don't forget I have deadly aim."

Colby swung into a parking spot, the engine died, doors popped open and McKaslin girls spilled into the pleasant evening sunshine.

"I just want to point out that this isn't far from home. Practically a stone's throw." Colbie fell in beside Brooke and hooked their arms together. "Or from the twins' place, if you decide to stay there. After all, Brianna will be getting married and Brandi will need another roommate. Just things to keep in mind."

Brooke rolled her eyes.

"That won't be for a while," Bree pointed out, walking beside her twin. "Right, Brandi? Max wants a winter wedding, I want a spring wedding—"

"—but if she wants to move in with us, say now, Bree and I can bunk together—" Brandi explained.

"—and Brooke can have the second bedroom," Bree finished.

"Ooh, I like that plan," Colbie pronounced as she yanked open the door. Noise, echoing in on itself, met them along with the breeze of air conditioning.

"Colbie and the twins," a rumbling voice— not Liam's—greeted them. A tall, blond, vaguely familiar-looking man strolled in from a nearby office, a referee's whistle hanging from his neck. "Can't believe you're here, especially with the trial going on."

"We felt the need to blow off steam," Bree spoke up.

"Plus I'm trying to talk Brooke into moving here and she likes to volunteer. What better place than here?" Colbie squeezed Brooke's arm a little harder. "Can you help me with my plan?"

"Maybe." The man had a friendly smile. "So you are the long-lost McKaslin girl. I'm Chad Lawson. I'm married to your cousin Rebecca. I'm also in charge here. Can't believe they gave me that much responsibility."

"Neither can we," Colbie quipped, leaning in closer to add, "He's the assistant youth pastor at our church, which is why he might look a little familiar."

"Glad to have you." He smiled. "The locker rooms are to your right, the rec rooms are to your left and if you're dying to play volleyball just follow the noise." Someone called Chad's name and he glanced over his shoulder.

"Gotta go. Duty calls." He jogged away, blowing his whistle, the sound reverberating in the cavernous building.

"Well, I'm heading for the locker room." Brandi held out her hand. "Give me your stuff. I'll lock it up."

"Thanks." Colbie handed over her purse and keys. Brooke held up her hands, showing she had nothing on her. She'd come ready to play.

She couldn't say why her pulse skipped a few beats as she let Colbie tug her into the gymnasium. Six games were in progress in the huge space, where teenagers along with a few adults leaped, spiked and served, dove for saves and cheered points earned. Brooke paused on the sidelines, soaking it in.

"Brooke, Colbie! Over here." A pleasant tenor rose above all the other sounds. Liam, with the ball tucked into the crook of his arm, waved his free hand over his head. Masculine. Athletic. Heartstopping. "I'm one player down."

"Go on," Colbie whispered to her. "I'm a terrible player. At least you won't be a laughingstock. Go on, go."

"I'm not fooled." She knew what her sister was up to, but did it matter? Not a bit. No ploy of Colbie's to match her up with Liam could possibly work. And why? Because she'd made up her mind. Her heart was invincible.

"Why don't you take the spot next to me?" He looked like a natural—feet braced, hair tousled. "That way I can give you a few pointers if you need 'em. Everyone, this is Brooke. Brooke, this is everyone. Are you ready to play?"

"Might as well." She slipped into the back row beside him, nodding in greeting to the friendly teenage faces turning to smile at her. Across the net the opposing team took their stances, fight faces on.

"It'll be fun, you'll see." Liam popped the ball out of the crook of his arm, took position and punched out a perfect serve. The white orb sailed over the net in a streak. Opponents scrambled to set and spike it and another pounded it home.

"How much do you know about the game?" he asked as a front-line teen pummeled the ball back over the net.

"A little. I haven't played since my high school days." She kept her eye on the ball as an opponent rushed, knelt and saved it. Teammates rushed in to help.

"The skills will come back to you." He planted his feet, light on his heels, ready in case he had to make a save. "The important thing is to have fun."

"Right. That's why I'm here." The ball sailed across the net with a fierce trajectory, whizzing straight at the gym floor. He sprang, already figuring he'd have to dive for this one when a slender, lithe form slid in front of him, arms out and clasped, skidding across the polished wood. The ball hit her exposed forearms with a slap and sailed into a perfect arc. Jen from the front row leaped to beat it over the net. The ball smashed into the floor. Score!

"Way to go, Brooke!" Jen called out, joined in by the others. "Great save."

Speechless, Liam's jaw hung open as he watched the prim and proper Miss Brooke McKaslin swipe a flyaway tendril out of her eyes, plant the heel of her hand on the floor and shrug. "You made the point. That was awesome."

"I won't argue," the teen said charmingly, obviously instantly liking Brooke.

Who wouldn't? He held out his hand, clasped hers and ignored the jolt that bolted straight to his soul. He breathed in her light vanilla fragrance as he helped her onto her feet. "So, you know a little about the game?"

"Okay, so I was on my high school team and we took state. Twice." Her pigtails bobbed, framing her heart-shaped face, making her endearing. No one could be cuter as she caught the ball one-handed.

"And you didn't think to mention this earlier?" He arched one brow, easing into place at the end of the front row.

"I wanted it to be a surprise."

A surprise? How about a bombshell? He shook his head, trying to get into the game as she served like a pro. The ball zipped over the net like a missile. The woman was more than a mystery.

And wasn't that a problem?

"I hope you can come on Saturday, too." Jen swiped sweat from her forehead as she gave the ball a toss. Chad, standing at the sidelines, caught it handily. Only one game was still going on and most kids were heading toward the locker room or the front door.

"Yeah, you rocked," Krys agreed, dreadlocks

bobbing. "You've got to show me how you serve like that. It was killer."

"An instant score half the time." Sofia joined the others. The small group of teenage girls surrounded her. "I want to learn the secret, too."

"I'll show you what I can." Personally, she didn't think her serve was all that great, but it was nice to feel she could help out. "You have a fantastic spike, Sofia. And, Krys, you were the top scorer."

"Come on Saturday." Jen squeezed her arm before leading the others, too.

"You're popular." Liam ambled up behind her, hands on his hips. Magnificent. Why couldn't she think of another word, any word, to describe him?

Probably because no other word would do. Tousled hair, damp with sweat, his gray T-shirt untucked, muscles bunching.

Magnificent wasn't her thing. Unmoved, she swiped a bead of sweat off her forehead. "Everyone's being nice."

"No, those girls like you. You made an impression on them."

"Only because of my serve." She wasn't going to acknowledge his compliment. He couldn't get past her barriers, not even with kindness. "It's a great group of kids here. I like them, too."

"Most of them are at risk. Some have already gotten into a lot of trouble. Jen's on probation, and Krys is just out of juvy. This is a good place for them to spend their time, learn about God and build their self-esteem. Good game tonight, Kent." He paused to high-five a teenage boy who dashed by. "Then again, I'm biased. I believe in this program."

"I can see why." Emotion lodged beneath her windpipe, realizing just how much she and those girls had in common. The wish to help them rose up within her, but she couldn't tell Liam that.

"I saw a lot when I was traveling the world. So much suffering. I'm just one man. What's that against all that pain?" He shrugged, scattering thick, dark locks of hair.

It was easy to see the good in him—so much good. He genuinely seemed to care for others, for doing what was right.

Don't even think about softening your stance, she told herself, bracing her feet, fisting her hands. "Surely you made some difference as a reporter."

"It wasn't enough. I've been in Haiti, Afghanistan, the Sudan. I've reported on famines, civil wars, earthquakes and genocide."

"I hadn't realized you'd done so much."

"No, I didn't do anything. I was just there as a witness."

He stopped in front of a row of vending machines and dug into his pocket. "It felt like the problems were already too big. All I could do was tell people about it. I couldn't try to fix it."

"I can't imagine how that affected you. To see all that close up and personal."

"It put my life into perspective. That's why I volunteer. It's the personal level, when you give of yourself and your heart that makes a real difference. Every little bit helps." He plugged coins into the machine. "Which soda?"

"Oh, I can get my own." She ducked her chin, blushing slightly.

"I need to push a button. Tell me which one. Diet, right?" He waited, she nodded and the can slid down the chute.

"Do you regret giving up that kind of career?"

"No. When my Grandfather Knightly got sick, nothing else mattered. There are days I miss it, but I have a real chance to help out my grandfather. When I was growing up he made sure I had everything I needed to be the kind of man I wanted to be. That's no small gift he gave me." He knelt to fetch the ice-cold can. When he handed it over, her soft fingers brushed his. He gritted his teeth but he couldn't stop the impact jolting through him, soul deep.

"I'm sure he feels the same way about you." She popped the top, thanked him for the soda and took a dainty sip.

He added a few more coins and waited for his cola to plunk down. There he was sharing again, but was she?

No, she held back. Quiet, reserved, walls up. Her stories were her business, he respected that, but he couldn't ignore the jolt still alive in his soul. He was attracted to her. The last woman he'd cared about had been a closed book, hiding so much of herself and he'd blithely accepted that, determined to gain her trust.

Big mistake. The betrayal still clung like a stain he couldn't wash out. He'd fallen in love with someone who hadn't existed. Someone who'd made him believe one thing when she was the polar opposite. He wouldn't make that mistake again, so why was he sharing so much?

Frustrated, he popped the top and listened to the symphony of carbonated bubbles echoing inside the can. Time for him to be remote, too.

"Helping Pop run the paper keeps me busy." He took a sip of cold soda, let it slide across his tongue and cool him on the way down. He looked around. "I'm not sure what happened to your sisters."

"Oh, I see them." She peered into a dark room where a movie was playing on a screen. "They're watching a show."

"I see Colbie ducked in there. It should be over in a minute. Thanks for coming by." He hesitated a moment, wondering if he ought to leave her, but needing to for his own well-being. He headed to the outside door, where Chad and another pastor were talking seriously with a small circle of teenagers.

"Wait."

Her soft call spun him around. She took a step toward him. "I never asked how Oscar liked day care."

"They tell me he howled for the first hour and then ran nonstop playing his heart out for the rest of the day." His shoes carried him a few steps toward her when he'd meant to head away. "Oscar was having so much fun playing in a wading pool that it took him a few minutes to notice I'd come to pick him up."

"Then it was a hit."

"A major one. Oscar needs a little more training. I probably do, too."

"When do you want me to come by?"

"Tomorrow works for me." He took another sip, keeping his gaze down, keeping it light. Brooke was good for Oscar and she needed the job.

"Great." She smiled, looking a little awkward and a little lost. She opened her mouth as if she wanted to say something more but stayed silent. Uncertain.

It was better to keep distance firmly between them. He fought the urge to try to cross it, held up his soda can as a goodbye and walked away.

Liam's story about what he'd seen traveling the world had touched her. It moved her. Thinking of the world's suffering he'd witnessed, she wanted to know more of his story. But she hadn't asked, afraid her steel defenses might buckle again.

"Good night. That was totally fun." Brandi swooped in to hug her tight in Lil's shadowed front yard. "I'm not into volleyball, but the movie was great. If you need someone to go with you next time, say the word."

"Me, too." Bree squeezed in, hugging them both.

"Me, three. Group hug." Colbie shouldered her way in. A real sister moment. This was what she'd been missing living two states away. The realization roped her in, making it hard to let go when the twins bobbed backward. Colbie kept a tight hold on her, though, as if she didn't plan on letting go. Bless her.

"Tell Lil good-night for us." Bree excavated her keys from her purse. "Thanks for putting up with us."

"You two are no hardship." Colbie waved with her free hand. "Drive safe and all that."

"Will do." Bree bopped into the truck and started the engine. The window whizzed down. "See you tomorrow."

"Count on it." Brooke adored her sisters. She alone knew how hard it was to sit in a courtroom waiting for justice. Her stomach clenched up tight, a little worried for Bree.

"Bye!" The little truck motored away, taillights glowing in the darkness.

"I can't believe how well she's doing." Colbie watched them go. "I would be a basket case if I had to sit in court and look at the men who shot me, but she's a rock."

"She's awesome." Brooke ambled alongside her sister up the dim pathway. Grasses rustled in the breeze and lilacs sent fragrance wafting their way. "I wish I had her strength."

"Are you kidding? That's the same thing she told me about you before the trial started." Colbie tripped along, dark hair bobbing with her gait. "I can't believe the way you've put your life together from scratch. You had to start all over again. With nothing. Not one thing."

"My life isn't as together as you think, not even close." Sweet of her sister to try to buoy her up like that, but honestly. "What little I own is in a storage unit in south Seattle. My job included quarters at the halfway house. When I was let go, I lost my room."

"Oh, sorry, I was wrong. You are completely pathetic." Gentle love shimmered in her words as she slung an arm over Brooke's shoulders, belying her words and saying so much more. "Do you know what this is?"

"I'm afraid to guess."

"Divine intervention, sister mine. A big neon

sign shining from heaven flashing, 'Move to Montana, move to Montana.'"

"Colbie, I'm starting to sense a recurring theme." Brooke laughed, climbed the stairs and breathed in the lovely fragrances of the night, of home.

"A girl has to try. You are loved here, Brooke. You know that, right?"

"It's occurring to me. Back at ya." All those years when she'd been young and had not known Colbie or the twins haunted her now—nothing but wasted time. What if Lil hadn't begun corresponding with her when she was in jail? Lil's generosity had changed her life. Gratitude welled up, too great for any words to describe. For the first time in a long while she felt a part of something, a part of her family.

"Girls, there you are." Lil hit Pause on the remote and the crime scene drama froze on the screen.

"Howdy." Luke, seated on the couch, lurched to his feet. At six-three he dominated the small living room. "Looks like it's time for me to skedaddle. I've got longer than an hour's drive."

"Sure you won't stay the night?" Lil asked.

"Thanks, but Hunter would have my hide. Wakeup is at four on the farm. He wouldn't be pleased with me if I wasn't there to help with the chores. Again." He pulled keys from his pocket. "See you around, you two. Keep out of trouble."

"Who, us?" Colbie's hand flew to her chest, sounding innocent. "You know me. I'm never trouble."

"Of course you're not." Luke winked, kissed Lil on the cheek and ambled over. "Brooke, you're smiling."

"What? I've been known to smile from time to time."

"Sure, but you look happy. It's good to see." He grabbed his Stetson from the closet shelf and ambled by. "You keep on being happy, okay?"

"I'll try. What about you?"

"I run a dairy with Hunter. How happy can I be?" he quipped, winking, hiding the affection he felt for their taciturn brother. "See you tomorrow."

"Bye." She closed the door after him, already missing him.

"Did you have a good time tonight?" Lil's question drew her back.

"Moderately." As if she wanted to open that can of worms. She knew exactly where Lil was heading. Time to change the subject. "Did you know your daughter is a terrible volleyball player?"

"I've heard rumors but I haven't wanted to believe it," Lil quipped. "At least you got Colbie out tonight. Colbie, see how I'm just fine? Luke and I had a great time."

"Good. I don't trust just anyone to stay with you." Colbie dropped into the overstuffed chair next to her mom and gestured toward the TV screen. "No, don't rewind it. Just catch me up. How is their romance going? I can't wait until she figures out that he loves her."

"Then keep watching." Lil pressed the remote, the actors on the screen burst into motion and the accord between mother and daughter emanated with deep and comfortable affection. "Brooke, are you going to join us? This is the best part. They're about to catch the killer."

"So I see." She set down her things and moseyed closer but it wasn't the show that held her attention. It was Colbie as she searched her mother's face and smoothed a hair out of place, worry frowning her forehead. Despite appearances it hadn't been easy for Colbie to leave her mom tonight. Even with Luke keeping an eye on her.

The action on the TV intensified, the cops made an arrest and justice was ensured.

"Look right there." Lil pointed to the screen. "That poignant look between them."

"Oh, he knows." Colbie sighed, pleased. In the lamplight, dark circles bruised her skin, revealing her exhaustion. "Ooh, next week's episode is going to be good."

"You know it." Lil leaned back into her chair as the evening news came on. The lead story? The Backdoor Burglars trial. Colbie reached forward and flicked it off.

"I'd rather end the day on a good note," she explained with a shrug. "Time to get you ready for bed, Mom. We have another big day ahead."

"I'll do it." Brooke seized the grips of Lil's wheelchair. "Don't even think about arguing. I love Lil. I want to spend time with her. I'm just selfish that way."

"Dear, I feel the same way about you." Pleased, Lil bent forward to release the brake.

Colbie knelt to do it. "I'm not letting you get away that easily. Brooke is our guest. She should be lounging on the couch."

"Is she always that bossy?" Brooke winked, pulling the wheelchair back with her.

"She thinks she's in charge. Poor, misguided Colbie." Lil's eyes twinkled. "Honey, I recorded a few sitcoms you missed earlier. Why don't you put your feet up and watch them?"

"Yeah, Colbie. If you sit and stay, I'll give you a cookie." She couldn't resist teasing. "It works for Oscar."

"It depends. What kind of cookie?" Colbie laughed, but the appreciation in her gaze said something more.

Brooke hoped hers said something, too, as she turned Lil around. She had no idea how Colbie managed everything on her own—her mother's care, supporting them both, making sure Lil had everything she needed. What time did that leave

Colbie for herself? Brooke suspected tonight's outing was a rare occurrence.

It was for her, too. She'd had fun. And Liam? He clung to the back of her mind, refusing to budge.

Chapter Nine

"No, I'll park the car." Brooke stole the Toyota's keys from Colbie faster than a pickpocket. Success. She ignored her sister's disapproving look, kissed Lil on the cheek and hooked her purse higher on her shoulder. "Colbie, you go in and get settled first for a change. I'll go in search of a parking spot."

"It's crowded this morning," Lil trilled, reaching out to take Bree by the hand. "How are you doing, dear? Are you ready for this?"

"They may not get to the testimony about Juanita's death today. We'll see." Bree gulped, chin up, all composure. Good to see her so strong, but tough to know how she had to feel deep inside. Max pulled her into his sheltering arms and she managed a determined smile. "All that matters is I'm not alone. With you guys here, I can do anything."

"I'm right by your side, gorgeous." Max, a protective and strong man, brushed a kiss on Bree's forehead.

Bree deserved no less.

See, there are good and honest men out there, Brooke told herself as she hopped behind the wheel. Men who didn't let a woman down; men who didn't use them for their own gain. Her brothers were that way, two men sworn to walk the right path in life. Why wasn't it easier to believe there were more guys like that out there?

It was totally her perspective. She buckled up, put the SUV in gear and waited for a break in traffic. Or maybe it was her experience that made her quick to judge and leap to the wrong conclusions.

Don't think about Liam, she told herself as she pulled away from the curb in front of the courthouse and maneuvered into the street. *Do not think about the man who played killer volleyball, who made you feel welcome in a group of strangers and who obviously was respected and liked by a gym full of teenagers.* She couldn't help but notice how many kids talked to him, high-fived him and looked up to him.

Don't do it, Brooke. She kept her gaze firmly on the road ahead of her, where her thoughts ought to be. She signaled, squinted against the sun, noticed the few handicapped spaces in the lot were filled and kept going. Her phone rang, buried in the depths of her purse. She couldn't dig for it so she kept going, wondering if it was Liam. They hadn't agreed on a time for Oscar's training today.

Liam. She grimaced, frustrated with herself. Why couldn't she stop thinking about that man? She had defenses to keep fortified and she couldn't do that if she thought too hard about how he'd opened up to her last night.

She spotted a space along the curb and swung into it awkwardly. She relied on the bus in Seattle, so her parallel parking skills were just a tad rusty. First she jimmied back and then forward, spun the wheel all the way to the left and back to the right. Wheels bumped the curb. Oops, a little too far. She jimmied a little more and leaned across the front seat to open the passenger door. Appropriately close to the curb.

Whew. Her parking skills could only get better from here and at least this was one less thing Colbie had to do. She pulled the parking brake, grabbed her purse and dug by feel. Lip gloss, hairbrush, phone. She plucked it out, trying to pretend she wasn't anxious to see who was listed on her screen.

Not Liam because the number had an Oregon area code. Could it be about a job? Anticipation shook through her as she dialed her voice mail. This had to be good news, right? Or why else would they bother to call?

"Miss McKaslin, I'm Ellen Chambers. I would

like to schedule an interview in the next few weeks." A pleasant, no-nonsense voice paused and paper shuffled. "I'm quite pleased with your experience. You are just the person we are looking for in our program. I hope I hear from you."

Yes! She saved the message, raised her arms in victory and laughed out loud. Things were looking up. Maybe she wouldn't be unemployed for much longer. Woo-hoo. She dropped the phone in her purse, unhooked the seat belt and a knock on the window scared her to death.

"Dad." The word squeaked out of her tight throat. Joy drained from her in an instant. Air puffed out of her lungs, leaving her shocked as she stared at the ragged, unkempt man on the other side of the glass.

"Brookie." The withered person was a pale imitation of the man she remembered. He hauled open the SUV's door. "Thought you were Colbie until I got up close. Why, girl, I haven't seen you since your trial."

"I remember." She could still hear the last thing he'd said to her in the courtroom after her conviction. *Guess this is goodbye. It wouldn't look good for me to be caught hanging around with a felon, even if it is my daughter.*

"What are you doing here?" She slipped from the seat. Her feet hit the pavement so hard, the impact ricocheted up her legs and her teeth clacked together. "I thought Hunter and Luke told you to stay away from the trial."

"Sure, sure, I know. I was just passing by. I'm concerned about my girl in there." His bushy brows frowned. His hair had gone gray and his face was hollow. "Been following it on the news. It just isn't right. I ought to be with family. That's why I came back here after I was released."

"Your being here upsets Bree. It hurts Lil." She couldn't muster up anger at her father, at the sad old man he'd become. But that didn't mean she would lower her guards against him. "You need to go."

"I thought you would understand out of everyone, Brooke." Mick McKaslin shut the door for her and trailed her around the back of the vehicle. "You know how hard it is to get on your feet after doing time. No one wants to hire an ex-con."

"Are you in a program, Dad?" She stepped onto the sidewalk, heavy inside. It hurt to remember the vibrant, charming father he'd been when she was little, when her family had been whole. He opened his mouth to argue, but she stopped him. "Don't even think about lying to me. You smell like whiskey."

"You lost him, too. I shouldn't have to tell you what that does to a man to bury his son." He swiped his face with his hand, a little dramatic. Probably working up to ask her for money.

"Don't bring up Joe's death." She could barely stand to think about the younger brother she'd lost. No one in the family could endure mentioning it. It hurt too much. "Don't you blame this on him."

"I didn't even get to go to the funeral. I was locked up." He gulped in air, thin, worn, his handed-down clothes a few sizes too large and badly wrinkled. Probably he'd slept in them. "You know how it was. You were also behind bars when it happened. When he died."

Why did he have to keep mentioning it? It was too much. Not even the steel walls around her heart could withstand the pressure. Memories rushed in like water through a crack in a levee, rushing forward, bringing more with it. Time reeled backward and she was in the prison courtyard with the summer sun burning on her back and splashing across Lil's flowery script, feeling the rock of grief hurl into her. She hadn't attended the funeral. "Stop it, Dad. I don't want to remember."

"What? You're too good to hurt? Think you're better than your old man?" Mick McKaslin's face twisted, quick to anger. Every life's blow had driven him lower in life, when he'd been raised better than this. She didn't know why he'd made the choices he had, but he didn't look like a man dedicated to changing. He scowled, his tone scolding. "I expected more from you. You've been locked up. Remember when that jury turned on you?"

"You need to go, Dad." Her stomach tumbled. Sweat popped out on her forehead. Something in her chest began to collapse. Maybe it was her heart. She jammed her fist into her bag, desperate to find her phone before the memories hit. She tried to breathe but couldn't find any oxygen nor could she stop the images from rising up. Once again she could feel the fluorescent lights beaming down on her as she stood beside her attorney. The verdict rang out in the silent courtroom.

Guilty. The rush of her denial, the shock racing through her system, the sound of her mother's sobs battered her. When the truth had sunk in and she'd realized that they hadn't believed her, her knees gave out and she collapsed into the chair at the defense table. Shattered. She shook her head but the memory clung to her.

"You need to go, Dad." The words tore out of her. "You upset everyone and you do it on purpose. And no, don't even think about asking for money."

"I didn't expect you to turn on me, too." He might act sorrowful but that wasn't the emotion glinting in his eyes. His jaw worked angrily. "You and me, we're just alike, Brookie, two ex—"

A footfall sounded behind her, followed by a man's booming voice. "Is there a problem here?"

"Liam." She choked, terrified, relieved and embarrassed. What had he overheard, or had he been too far away?

"Looks like you're having a little trouble. Hi, Mick." Authority boomed in Liam's voice. "You'll be moving along, right?"

"Just saying howdy to my daughter. There's no law against that." Mick's chin went up, defensive, but he edged back a few paces. "I moved here to be close to my kids. This not being able to see them ain't right."

"It's what your kids want." Liam stood by her side, loyal.

"Get into a program, Dad. Sober up. Nothing is going to change between all of us until you do." Shame shadowed her as she spun on her heels and hit the sidewalk, not seeing where she was going, her gasps grating her throat like sobs. How much had Liam heard? Why had she let the past get the best of her? It was over and gone. She had to stop letting it have the power to hurt her so much.

"Brooke?" A deep-noted voice rumbled with concern. His footsteps tapped behind her on the sidewalk, closing in. Liam.

Again.

She stopped and squeezed her eyes shut, dreading what he might say. His shoes tapped hollowly against concrete, her skin tingling as he drew nearer.

Her pulse skipped and her soul whispered in reaction. She opened her eyes to his reassuring presence.

"Are you all right?" His words threatened to soothe her. His tone vibrated richly, dipping deeply, comforting. If he'd heard her conversation with Dad, then he wouldn't be looking at her that way. Like he cared. "I've heard from Gram how your dad can be. I also remember my Grandfather Knightly mentioning that he covered Mick's arrest and trial years back."

"I'm sorry you had to see that." She'd never seen kinder eyes. They warmed like the sky at noon, bluer than dreams and full of honest caring. It would be so easy to tumble, to let down her guards and lean on him. Her chest twisted tight with an emotion she couldn't name.

"I've seen worse." Gentle humor tugged at the corners of his mouth. "I told Mick to move on or your brothers and I would help him. No one wants Bree or Lil upset, not today."

"Court's in session by now. You're missing testimony."

"Roger will fill me in." He shrugged his dependable shoulders and laid one hand on the small of her back. He swallowed hard at the surprising zing of pure emotion. The comfortable distance between them vanished and he felt too close, but could he move away?

No. Brooke was hurting. Pain shone in her eyes and somehow arrowed into his heart. That was a problem. He cleared his throat, trying to dislodge that pesky emotion. "I'm more concerned about you."

"No, I'm okay." She lifted her chin, strain telegraphing through her. He could feel her muscles bunched beneath his palm.

"You don't look okay."

"It was nice of you to intervene." She bit her bottom lip, still trembling, unguarded. Giving him a glimpse of the real Brooke she worked so hard to protect.

"Least I could do for the woman who taught Oscar to sit." He smiled, battling a wash of gentleness filling him.

"You could have taught him if you would have bought a dog book or watched a TV show on dog training." Some of the tension eased beneath his hand. She tilted her head, gazing up at him, those shutters slipping back in place.

But she couldn't pretend she hadn't been hurting or that he hadn't seen.

"True." He couldn't argue with her or ignore the weakening around his heart.

Don't go soft for the woman, he tried to tell himself. He'd be smart to hold his ground and reinstate distance between them. Except it was hard to ignore the pain he'd seen in her.

"Don't worry, Mick's almost to the end of the block."

He glanced down the street, watchful. He knew an addict when he spotted one. Drugs and alcohol took their cost from a person. He knew at least part of the story. A proposal to Lil that Mick had never made good on while he'd still been married—a terrible discovery for Lil who found out the truth too late. Another marriage to the twins' mother, ending in divorce. Time served on a counterfeiting charge. Life on the streets.

Brooke deserved a better father than that. Liam's hand remained on her shoulder. She wasn't alone. He wanted her to know that. "He's turned the corner. He's gone."

"For now." Worry moved across her heart-shaped face, crinkling the corners of her eyes and tugging down her pretty mouth.

Not that he should be noticing how pretty her mouth was, soft and expressive. As lush as newly blooming roses in June.

"I'm worried about Bree seeing him. And Lil. She gets so upset." Another piece to the puzzle of Brooke McKaslin. Even terribly upset, she was quick to care about others. Hard not to be touched by that.

"He didn't look good." He steered her forward.

He guided her off the curve and pulled her to his side. She felt slight against him, just a fragile slip of a woman, all sweetness and heart. He swallowed against the feelings building in his chest, refusing to let them rise. "Is he homeless?" Liam asked.

"Staying at a shelter, I think. We've all been burned by him so many times, we've had to cut ties."

"It's called self-preservation." And it would definitely be self-preservation to pull away from her now and put a little distance between them. But did he?

No. Warmth crept into his chest as he saw her safely across the street. *This isn't tenderness,* he told himself. He was just being a gentleman, that was all. He didn't want to start caring about her.

Please don't let this tenderness I feel for her grow, Lord, he prayed for good measure. "Dad wasn't always like this." Brooke looked at him, drawing him in with some sort of gravitational pull and made the warm feeling in his chest rear up.

It's not caring, he told himself stubbornly.

"He used to be kind and funny and an involved dad when Hunter, Luke, Joe and I were very young." She stepped out of his arms naturally, stepping onto the curb.

His hand felt empty. He was hollow without her at his side. "Joe?"

"My younger brother. He's gone now." Hard to

miss the grief jumbling up her words. She hung her head and took a deep breath. The pain was still fresh.

"That's right. I was overseas at the time. Gram told me." He stepped slightly ahead of her, nearing the coffeehouse's front door. "It was years ago."

"Yes. Joe's death hit all of us hard, but Dad's clearly gone into another downward spiral. Maybe that's why, maybe not." Joe, a firefighter for the state, had lost his life battling a wildfire. He'd been the best of all of them, good and stalwart and full of promise. "Truth is, my mom spiraled, too."

"You don't talk about her much."

"We're not close." How did she begin to talk about why, especially after seeing her father? She tried not to think of all the letters she'd written in prison to her mom that had come back marked "Return to sender." "These days Lil is more of a mom to me."

"You couldn't do better. I'm glad you have her."

"Me, too." His gaze searched hers as if he could see glimpses of her secrets, seeing so deeply in that her instincts shouted to turn away. But did her feet budge? Not a chance. And why was her heart galloping as if she'd run ten miles? She cleared her throat, caught by him. "Thanks for being here. For listening."

"It's what friends do." He tugged open the shop door, waiting for her to enter.

"That's what we are? Friends?" Her feet managed to carry her forward into the bustling shop.

"Yep, friend. One hundred percent. You might as well put me on speed dial."

"Wow, that's just what I was trying to avoid." She breathed in the comforting scent of coffee.

"Sorry to break this to you, but you're stuck with me for now."

"I don't have a choice?" She eased into the back of the line at the counter.

"Not really. You've got a little color back in your face. Feeling better?"

"For now." She glanced over her shoulder at the crowded shop. She caught a glimpse of the street and a corner of the courthouse. How was Bree doing this?

"Is that why you live in Seattle?" He pulled out his wallet. "To stay away from your dad?"

"No. It's where I got a job." She studied the menu tacked on the wall behind the register. The truth spilled out of her. "I had a hard time finding work. A halfway house in Seattle was the only place offering, so I took it."

"You are in social work. I can see that." He tossed a casual grin at the clerk behind the counter. "I'll have a regular latte. How about you, Brooke?"

"A mocha. I can't say no to chocolate. I try but my will is weak." Social work? Guilt twisted through her. That sounded more elevated than her job had been doing basic cleaning and helping out in the office. But how could she tell Liam that? If he knew, he'd turn away and that was the last thing she wanted. She watched as the clerk rang up the sale. "It looks like I finally have a shot at a new job."

"That's great." He dropped all his change in the tip jar. "Any chance it's here in town?"

"No. Portland."

"Colbie is going to be crushed."

"She's not the only one. This place is starting to grow on me."

"I know the feeling. When my grandfather first got his diagnosis and I came back to help out, my foot was itching to get back on the road and pick up my old life. I loved what I did." He took the two cups from the barista with thanks and handed Brooke's over.

She did her best not to let their fingers touch. "Why did you end up staying?"

"When it came down to it, I didn't want to leave."

"I get that." She walked through the door he held for her, letting the sweet May sun shine on her face. She stopped, waiting for him as he held the door for two elderly ladies, standing there so strong and polite. Against her will her heart gave a little flutter.

Don't start thinking he's a gentleman, she told herself, but it was too late.

"I've always been comfortable staying away from here," she confessed when he joined her on the bustling sidewalk. "Living in Seattle made it easier to start over. To put my past behind me."

"There's only one thing that can make you want to pack up, leave town and start over." His gaze found hers, looking so deep she felt as if he could see everything. "I know because I almost did it."

"You did?" She swallowed hard. Had he somehow guessed the truth? What was he going to say?

Chapter Ten

"A relationship gone terribly wrong. That will make you want to leave town." He took a sip of coffee, his pace leisurely beside her, taking his time as the wind ruffled his hair. "Is that what happened to you?"

Relief left her hands too shaky to lift her cup. Maybe she should just tell him the truth, confess where she'd spent most of her twenties. But did the words come? No, they stuck in her throat, refusing to budge. "Yes, I did have a relationship go bad. I was living near Miles City at the time."

"He broke your heart?" Understanding radiated from him.

This man was dangerous. He could disarm her defenses with one caring look. Why couldn't she stop it? She took a tentative sip of the steaming hot drink. Chocolatey coffee sluiced across her tongue. "We met in our senior year of high school. Darren was the new kid in town. Charming, funny, he just grabbed everyone's attention. Even mine."

"He was your first love." Understanding layered his voice, as if he knew that particular malady.

"I fell so hard I didn't hold back a single piece of my heart. I didn't know any better." So easy to remember that wintry day when Darren Adams had driven her home after volleyball practice. "I thought he was wonderful, that he could do no wrong. Love makes you blind."

"It certainly can. Been there myself." He raised his cup in a salute. "How did he break your heart? Lie to you? Cheat on you? Marry someone else?"

"He hurt me. I had just turned twenty when the blinders came off with such force I haven't had a relationship since." She stepped off the curb and followed the sidewalk across the street.

"He really hurt you." She had to be a few years older than Colbie, so that put her in her late twenties. That was a long time for a woman to go without dating. Domestic violence, he figured. That had to be what happened, why sadness dimmed the brightness of her violet eyes. She brushed it off, shrugged her shoulders, making like it was no big deal.

But he knew. Whatever this force that connected them deepened, a tie between her spirit and his. She couldn't hide her disillusionment. So that was why she'd kept her distance and stayed closed off. She'd been really hurt. As much as he hated that, at least he understood. Tension eased behind his ribs, tension he hadn't even known was there.

"He deceived me." Pain strained her voice, although she fought to hide it. "He betrayed me. I'm not sure I ever got over it."

"I know the feeling. Sidney pretended to be an honest and trustworthy Christian, someone she wasn't."

"What happened?" She watched him with compassion so sincere he couldn't stop from opening up.

"I fell in love with her. Mostly through texts and phone calls because we were always on the move with our jobs, but we got together when we could. I think that's why I couldn't see what she was. I never got close enough, I never got to know her more deeply. She played a part and I wasn't around enough to question it."

"You blame yourself?"

"As much as I blame her. I should have seen she was just playing me. Just pretending to be sweet and kind when she wasn't like that at all. Not below the surface."

"How did you find out the truth?" She laid her hand on Liam's arm, a show of connection and empathy, so he didn't feel alone with his wounds.

"All that time, she made sure I saw her sweet side. Her fake side, as it turned out. After I moved here, I realized I was ready to settle down. I proposed, and she said yes. I flew out to meet her in Boston and we ran into her sponsor at a restaurant."

"Her sponsor?"

"Found out she was a recovering drug addict."

"Drugs?" The word felt torn from her.

"She had this entire other life I didn't know about. Part of the drug culture, a lifestyle she hadn't been able to let go of completely." He rubbed his hands over his face.

"You had to be devastated." Her heart beat so hard, she was sure it jarred her words. Drugs. Her hands started shaking, too.

"How could I marry her? There was this whole side of her I didn't know. She'd been lying all the time. Pretending to be wholesome as if she didn't have a past, as if she wasn't still struggling on and off with heroin addiction." He shrugged those big shoulders of his. Maybe determined to show that having his heart ripped out and his illusions destroyed was of little consequence to a tough guy like him.

She wasn't fooled. She wanted to reach out, but his story hit too close to her own.

"Darren was selling drugs on the side." Humiliation returned. She'd believed too easily. "I know how it feels to be lied to by the person you love most."

"Honesty is a trait I've come to admire in a woman. The best quality there is."

Why did her pulse skip guiltily? Because she was essentially doing the same thing as his ex. Showing him the woman she was now and not letting him know about the time in her life that marked her forever.

Memories threatened to engulf her, cold corridors, hopelessness, shattered dreams, but she wrestled them down, keeping them secret. What would he think if he knew the truth about her? If he knew of her conviction? He'd see his ex, that's what. There was no way now he would ever understand.

A tiny piece of hope died, one she hadn't even known was there.

Unaware of how she was thinking, Liam hauled open the courthouse door for her. Gorgeous man, strapping shoulders, kindness radiating through. The way the cheerful morning sun sifted over him, he looked like a fantasy. The problem with Liam was simple. He was a good man. Helpless against it, her iron defenses melted a little more. Maybe it didn't matter so much because there was no way she could open up to him now.

* * *

The morning's testimony had been difficult, so noon recess felt especially wonderful with the sun shining everywhere, blazing the street, the park and pedestrians with golden light. The moment her foot had hit the courthouse's front steps, she dreaded running into her dad again but he'd been nowhere in sight. Major relief. The hard part was telling Luke about it.

"Hunter is going to go ballistic when he hears." Luke pocketed his change and grabbed half the food bags and a drink carrier from the burger joint's counter. "You should have told us right away. This is unacceptable."

"I took care of it." She grabbed her share of the food and followed her brother to the door. "He's gone for now. Problem solved."

"You should have called one of us. I would have helped you." Luke shouldered open the door. "You didn't need to be alone with him."

"I wasn't alone with him." Liam slipped into her thoughts again. Pretending he hadn't, she sailed into the hot May day where the breeze flirted with nearby trees lining the sidewalks.

"Not alone, huh?" Luke grinned at that. "I guess this means Colbie's plot is working."

"Which one? The plan to talk me into moving to Montana? Or the plot to set me up with Liam?"

"Isn't that really the same strategy?" Luke chuckled, matching his pace with hers on the sidewalk. "If you have a boyfriend here, would you really want to move away?"

"It's a doomed plan. I have a job interview in two weeks." She'd returned Ms. Chambers's call after walking into the courthouse with Liam. She'd stood in the corridor, trying to hide her excitement while she scheduled an interview. The personnel lady had been especially encouraging. So, why did she feel a little down about it?

"Colbie and Lil are going to be crushed." Luke grinned in his easy, relaxed way. "They're sure you and Liam are going to start dating any minute."

"You need to stop listening to those matchmakers." Honestly. "Ever since Bree's engagement, they've been unstoppable."

"Nothing makes them happier than a wedding." Luke's dark blue gaze, full of amusement, met hers. "They're wondering who's next."

"Hey, don't look at me."

"You did come into court with Liam this morning. You're spending a lot of time with him."

"Sure, I'm training his dog."

"Yes, but I didn't see his dog this morning."

How did she explain not only was her heart off-limits to love, but after what she'd learned about Liam this morning, he would never be interested in a girl like her? In someone with her history. She ignored the unexplained clutch of pain in her heart. She kept her gaze glued to the sidewalk ahead of her and hoped her big brother wouldn't guess the truth. "There are absolutely no wedding bells in my future."

"Sure about that?"

"Absolutely, positively certain."

"That's too bad." Sympathy softened his voice. "I think you deserve someone nice after what happened to you."

Her throat closed up, making it hard to speak. Maybe it would be smart to change the subject. Throw the spotlight on him instead. "What about you? Are you dating anyone?"

"Me? Just who would I date?" He adjusted the drink carrier, shaking his head. "I live in the middle of farm country. I spend all day either on the tractor, in the barn or tending my cows."

"What about neighbors? People in town? How about church?"

"Neighbors are all married, far too old or far too young. As for the folks in town? Prospect is about a hundredth the size of Bozeman. I've got the same problem there as I do in church. Anyone who is single is too old, too young, not right at all or they've already turned me down."

"Have you tried the internet?" she quipped. "Desperate times call for desperate measures."

"Uh…" He fell silent, blushing profusely.

"You have?" She couldn't believe it. Her shy brother had ventured onto a dating site? "Do you have an online profile? How does that work? Do you do online chats with your matches?"

"No, it's nothing like that. I didn't try any of those dating sites." If he turned any redder, he might spontaneously combust. "I met someone on a website for readers. It's a site all about books."

"Oh, that makes sense." She didn't know anyone who read more than Luke did. "How did she catch your eye?"

"We both liked the same books. Over and over again we would post nearly the same comments. This one time in an online chat we started typing to each other. Hours passed and we didn't realize everyone else had left the chat room." He stopped at the corner, waiting for the light to change.

"I'm glad you've found someone, Luke. You're a good man." Proof that there were very good men in the world.

"Not that it's serious or anything. We're just friends." A muscle ticked along his jaw, as if maybe that wasn't the whole truth. "You won't tell anyone? You'll keep this secret?"

"For a price." She had to believe good things happened to good people. Luke certainly deserved someone to love him. "My lips are sealed. But if this does turn serious, I'd better be the first one you tell."

"Deal." The light changed and Luke took off, only slightly less red than he'd been.

The poor guy. She hugged the warm food bags to her, hurrying to keep up. Luke was a closed-off kind of man, shy when it came to personal things. It must have been hard for him to open up enough to admit his feelings.

She knew just how that felt.

The trees lining the park rustled cheerfully, shading the stretch of lawn. The grassy scent tickled her nose as a lazy bee droned by. Luke sidestepped to avoid the bee.

"Brooke!" Her name sailed on the wind. Colbie waved, leaving the twins, Hunter and Max to finish spreading out the blankets.

"We're coming, Colbie," Luke called out. "Don't break an arm. We see ya."

"You have to know we're starving here!" Colbie's laughter trilled like lark song as she leaped into action, all grace and bounce. "Yum, that smells good. There's nothing like burgers and fries. Hmm."

"Too bad we didn't get anything for you." Brooke couldn't resist teasing. "Sorry."

"Not funny. Don't get between a woman and her fries," Colbie quipped merrily. "I'm diabolical."

"Clearly." Brooke handed over one of the bags.

"I have a confession to make. I did something."

Colbie grabbed the bag and peered inside. No fries. "Brooke, care to guess what?"

"I can." Luke grinned dryly. "Does it have anything to do with the guy pushing Lil's chair?"

"What guy?" Brooke had a bad, bad feeling, the kind where the bottom of your stomach fell out and your knees buckled right before doom happened. She glanced around, saw Lil in her chair, fragile and adorable and grinning widely. And the strapping, towering hunk pushing her carefully from the parking lot to the grass could only be one man.

"Liam." Brooke had to blink twice, but the image of him remained. Stalwart, striking, laughing. The low rumble rang like music, deep and inviting. Everyone around her smiled in response. It took everything she had to keep the corners of her mouth appropriately straight.

"We ran into him on the sidewalk," Lil explained with a bob of her short dark hair as they walked straight toward the subject of their conversation. "We couldn't let him eat lunch all by himself."

"I couldn't say no." Liam easily manhandled the wheelchair over the uneven grass and stopped beside the blankets. "Lil charmed me, as she always does. Hi, again, Brooke."

"Hi." Her stomach swooped downward again like another sign of doom.

"Food!" Brandi bounded over to take charge of one of the drink containers.

"Fries!" Bree left Max's side and scooped one of the bags from Luke. "Just what I need. Fries can solve just about any problem."

"I'm sure there's some scientific study we can quote," Brandi agreed.

"Good thing there are a lot of fries. The testimony was grim this morning." Colbie circled around to hand over the food bag to Hunter. "It has to be horrible reliving all of that."

"I'm not sure how well I'm going to do on the stand. I'm praying I can keep it together. That's my goal." Bree unrolled the paper bag and dug out a wrapped cheeseburger, which she handed to Max. "The D.A. has been great. We've been going over and over my testimony and I feel comfortable with what I have to say. It's standing up for justice. Brooke, you know how important justice is."

"I do." She took a shaky breath, surprised at how casually Bree brought up the past, just like that, with no warning. Brooke swallowed, concentrated overly hard on extracting a cup of soda from the drink carrier and prayed she could keep her voice steady. "So many lives have been harmed by violence. You don't want any more lives hurt."

"Exactly. It's not about me anymore, but Juanita and the others who were killed that night." Bree handed out a second burger. "I'm feeling stronger. The post-traumatic stress is getting better."

"You're doing great, gorgeous." Max took her

hand and kissed it sweetly. Her engagement ring sparkled in the sunshine.

"You two. Ugh." Hunter rolled his eyes, too tough to fall for anything sappy. "Let me help with Lil, Liam."

"I've got her this time, thanks." Liam lifted Lil from her wheelchair. Hard not to notice those strong, muscled arms and gentleness as the big man cradled the fragile woman, lowering her onto the blanket with care.

Don't soften your stance on this guy, she told herself. *Don't do it.*

"So, I know it's too early." Colbie rushed over to help Lil get settled. "But any thoughts on a wedding date?"

"We're keeping that top secret," Max quipped, turning toward Bree as she sat down beside him, adorable with her light blond hair and charm.

"I do have a day in mind." Mysterious, Bree nudged her twin with her arm. "Don't guess. I know you can."

"Ooh, a challenge. Let me see. What day could it be?" Brandi scrunched up her face, just as adorable, the two so identical you couldn't tell the difference unless you knew them well.

The twins were fun to watch, but so were Colbie and Lil for an entirely different reason.

"You fuss too much, Colbie dear." Lil's alto held a note of love. "I'm just fine. Sit and relax."

"I can't help it, Mom." Colbie gave a lap blanket a firm shake and let the fleece settle over Lil's legs. "What else do you need?"

"I've got everything I need." Lil brushed Colbie's chin with a loving hand. "Now sit down. Didn't I raise you to obey your mother?"

"Sure, but I'm all kinds of trouble." Colbie pulled a cloth hat out of the bag behind Lil's chair and shaped it carefully before placing it on her mother's head to block the sun. Finally done, she slipped onto the blanket beside her mother. "Go on, Liam, sit down."

"It doesn't feel right being here without Oscar." He took the only available space left, which was next to Brooke. The importance was not lost on him. Colbie winked, clearly pleased her plan worked.

And he knew why. Colbie smiled at Brooke with the same loving attention she showed her mother. Brooke had been hurt by a boyfriend she loved and trusted. She was afraid to get hurt again. He knew exactly how that felt. It was good to have another piece of the puzzle because with one look into her soulful violet eyes, he saw a kindred spirit. He hunkered in beside her, wishing he didn't feel emotionally closer to her than ever.

She hooked his heart with that tentative smile. He couldn't deny it.

"Last time we were at this park, Oscar was running like a wild thing. Remember?" A weaker man might get lost in her violet-blue gaze. "He loved that Frisbee."

"He ran and ran and he never tired out. I couldn't believe it."

"I'm thinking he would make a good jogging buddy, except…"

"Except he doesn't heel," Brooke finished his thought, reached into the last food bag and handed him the last burger. "We could work on that tonight, if you want."

"Great. I didn't go running this morning. Just didn't want to leave him penned up in that kennel." He took the burger, his fingers brushed hers and the world stilled. Light and color, sound and motion all faded until there was only her. Just Brooke and the breeze in her dark hair, the sun kissing her lovely face and the stillness she put in his soul.

"You'd rather be with him than without him." Her quiet words spoke exactly what he felt.

How did she know? He swallowed hard, pulse rocketing through him because he didn't want to think about why. He didn't want to open up to another woman. He wasn't ready, he was fine on his own, he wasn't looking for a woman to shred his heart. Especially one about to leave town as soon as the trial was done.

Logic didn't stop his feelings and caring for her deepened ever further.

"Are you kidding? I'm too tough to get hung up

on a dog." Denial was the best course of action, he decided. "I'm glad I have him, but he's just a dog."

"Understatement of the century." She refused to be fooled by him, apparently. "Don't worry. I won't let your secret out. I won't tell that you're best friends with a dog."

"It's not my fault." Uh-oh, the woman was onto him. She'd figured him out. He straightened his spine, drawing himself up as imposingly as he could. "It's the dog's fault."

"He forced you to fall in love with him."

"Exactly. I'm a totally innocent man. I was a victim." Laughter bubbled in his chest and spread through him.

"Don't worry, I understand. The dog is to blame. Not you."

"I'm glad someone gets it. I don't want to wreck my hard-earned…"

"Reputation," she said, her soft alto blending with his like music.

Like perfect harmony.

"Uh, hello?" Colbie's voice came from what seemed like a galaxy away. "You two? Earth calling Brooke and Liam."

"What?" He shook his head, felt the wind on his cheek and looked around. He saw a circle of people watching with smirks on their faces. Funny, he'd forgotten they were there.

"We're waiting on you two," Bree spoke up. "To say grace? Or should we just go on without you…"

"And let you two keep flirting?" Brandi finished, beaming with delight.

"Flirting?" That was completely the wrong word. He would deny it with all of his might. "That's not what's going on here."

"No way. Are you kidding? This is what we do. Get wrapped up talking about Oscar." Brooke blushed. A wave of pink swept across her face.

Cute.

"It's Oscar's fault," he agreed. "Besides, she's his dog trainer. We need to have a certain…"

"Affinity?" Brooke came up with exactly the right word. "I don't want Oscar to have to go back to the pound if this doesn't work out between them."

"It's totally about Oscar," Liam agreed.

"Yeah, right. We see that." Colbie laughed, not buying it.

Neither was he.

"Dear Father," Lil began the blessing.

Liam bowed his head and folded his hands just in time.

Chapter Eleven

Images of Liam had stuck with her all afternoon. Impossible to get rid of them. In the courtroom she had concentrated as hard as she could on the rending testimony, but what was at the back of her mind? The rumbling richness of Liam's laughter, his presence beside her on the picnic blanket and the story about her past she hadn't told him. The one she could never tell him now.

After court had adjourned for the day, she'd run ahead to fetch the SUV and bring it curbside so Colbie could stay with Lil, but while she was sitting in traffic what popped into her head? Liam pushing Lil's chair over the grass, Liam gathering the delicate lady into his strong arms, Liam setting her gently on the blanket.

And now riding through the streets of Bozeman with Bree at the wheel, what was she thinking of? The fact that she couldn't wait to see him. She leaned her forehead against the window's glass, cool from the blast of air from the dashboard vents. What was wrong with her? Why had her defenses wobbled again?

"Are you worrying again?" Bree's gentle amusement rose above the radio belting out Christian music. "For the record, I'm glad you and Liam are getting along so well."

"It's all a show on my part," she quipped as the little pickup lumbered into a parking lot. "I'm just being nice to him for the money."

"Sure." Bree didn't look like she believed that for a moment. "It's all about the job with you, too."

"Right. It's all about Oscar." The truck puttered into the parking lot and rolled to a stop beneath the Dillard's Doggy Day Care sign. "I came all this way to spend time with you during the trial. To make sure you're okay. I'm not sure I should be spending evenings away like this. Maybe you need everyone to rally around you."

"I'm okay. I'm stronger than I ever thought." Exhaustion bruised the delicate skin beneath Bree's eyes, but she seemed stronger than ever. "Besides, you were with me today during that tough testimony. I can't tell you what it means. You were there for the hard part, so go have some fun tonight. I'll just be hanging with my fiancé and a sister or two."

"I could be one of those sisters." Her palms had

gone damp and she didn't want to think about why. Perhaps because at any moment a certain dog would be loping out of that building accompanied by a very handsome owner.

"You've been out of jail what, a year and a half?"

"Nineteen months."

"And how much fun have you had in that time?"

"Tons. So much I can't remember it all."

"Yeah, right." Bree reached across the console, her touch loving as her hand landed on Brooke's. "Have some fun tonight. Help Oscar. I don't want your visit home to be all about my trial."

"But that is the reason I'm here."

"Maybe it isn't. Who knows?" A mischievous look flashed in Bree's eyes. "Maybe God has led you here for another reason."

"To get closer to my sisters."

"Yes, but maybe there's another reason."

"To get closer to Lil."

"Really? Are you going to keep doing this? Do I have to spell it out?" Bree folded a lock of straight blond hair behind her ear. "Are you in denial about what's going on between you and Liam?"

"Nothing is going on between me and Liam." She refused to let it. It was as simple as that. If a girl wasn't in control of her heart, then what was she in control of?

"See? Denial. My point exactly." Bree chuckled, a light and happy sound. It was good seeing her little sister so alive. Brooke remembered how still Bree had been in ICU, fighting death. The beep of the monitors, the tubes and machines, the fear that she could slip away hovered in the room. Emotion clogged her throat and she swallowed. Did it budge? No, it remained, another image she couldn't erase.

"I can't imagine what you've been through." Bree turned serious, a loving sister who squeezed Brooke's hand. "I've thought a lot about it sitting in that courtroom and imagining what it was like for you to hear testimony against you, testimony that made you look guilty."

"It's in the past." She didn't necessarily want to talk about this subject, either. "There's nothing I can ever do to change it. I just have to go on and figure out how to make the best of where I am right now."

"That's what I've learned, too. It's helped to put the trial and getting shot in perspective. Tough times are a cruddy part of life but we can get through them. There are good and wonderful things on the other side."

"Like Max and your engagement ring?"

"Yes." Bree's diamond gleamed in the sunlight but not as brightly as the happiness on her face. "I'm praying so hard that the good waiting for you is greater than the hard times behind you."

"Ditto." She gave Bree's hand a squeeze, meaning it with her entire heart.

A resounding bark grabbed her attention. Oscar! A golden streak loped out the open door and into the parking lot.

"He's so cute," Bree cooed. "I can see why you like him."

"Oscar *is* adorable."

"Oh, I was talking about Liam." Bree laughed, apparently thinking it was so, so funny.

"Right." Brooke rolled her eyes, distracted by the thud of front paws hitting the side of the truck. A wet nose pressed against the glass and friendly chocolate eyes twinkled at her. His happy panting chased her worries away. "Hey, boy. Did you have fun today?"

A cheerful bark seemed to say, "Yes!"

If she concentrated on the dog, then she wouldn't have to notice the man. Even if she felt his approach like doom circling.

"Get down, you big clown." Liam's voice rang with humor as he tugged the big dog off the door. "No, I don't need any of your kisses."

Liam's laughter was a sound that lifted her soul.

Not going to fall for him. She gritted her teeth, steeled her spine and unhooked the seat belt. The man may have breached the outer layer of her shields, but she had plenty of defenses left in her arsenal.

"Have fun," Bree called out cheerfully. "Don't do anything I wouldn't do."

Honestly. Brooke rolled her eyes, shook her head and hopped onto the pavement. Bree drove off with a finger wave, her truck backfiring.

Deep rumbling laughter drew her attention. Oscar, prancing on both hind legs, kept trying to swipe Liam's chin with his tongue.

"Enough, dude! Down. C'mon." Laughter looked good on him. Liam tried to wrangle Oscar's paws off his chest. "Sure, I'm glad to see you, too, but can you get down, you big lug? Down. Sit."

Oscar gave one last kiss before he sank obediently to his haunches. His muscles quivered and he launched back up, unable to control himself, and landed another kiss along the side of Liam's face.

"Oh, you almost had it, buddy. Try it again. Sit." Liam could be a dream standing there, shoulders braced, tall, long and lean, dark good looks and sparkling blue eyes. He looked like everything dependable and trustworthy in a man, everything she once used to dream of. These days she wasn't a woman who could afford to dream. And if she did, no way could it be for Liam. This morning's conversation had made that undeniably clear.

"Sit for Brooke," Liam urged. "C'mon, you can do it. A little more. Good, good boy. You did it. Way to go!"

Think iron, Brooke. Unmovable steel. Don't let him get to you. She unclenched her teeth, relaxed her fists and risked a few steps closer to the pair. "Good job, Oscar. Good sit. Woo-hoo."

The dog's ears quirked. His head tilted. Delight glittered in his expressive eyes. Overjoyed, he rocketed off the ground with an explosive force NASA would be proud of. He leaped, he bounced, he danced with pride.

"I think that deserves a pizza." Liam hadn't gotten the full word out before Oscar barked enthusiastically, apparently putting in his two cents.

"See? He agrees. Two yay votes." Liam ambled over, way too handsome for her good. "What do you say? Will it be three yeses? Do we have a consensus?"

"What happens if I abstain?"

"Can you really say no to that face?" He gestured to the dog prancing at his side.

"No comment."

"Yeah, me, either." He whisked open the passenger door for her. Oscar, unable to wait his turn, flew into the front seat, bounded into the back and sat panting like a good boy, perhaps dreaming pizza dreams.

"How did the rest of the afternoon session go?" he asked, waiting as she stumbled closer.

"Very sad. The first waitress was on the stand, talking about what she saw." Another step took her to the truck, where he stood holding the door. So close she could see the strands of green threads in blue irises and the stubble of the day's growth beginning to darken his jaw. Air molecules popped and evaporated. He blocked her in, becoming all she could see. Every bit. No sky, no earth, nothing, just handsome man, wind-tossed dark hair and sincerity.

Why was she trembling? Why had her brain turned to mush? The effect of a long day. Surely that had to be it. When in doubt, cling to denial with both white-knuckled hands.

"C'mon. Hop in." He took her elbow and she planted one foot on the running board. *See, nothing to worry about.* That absolutely was not a sweet tingle of awareness at his touch. She felt nothing, nothing at all as she plopped onto the seat.

"Why didn't you stay in court all afternoon?" She tried to act casual because he wasn't affecting her in the least. Not a bit. "Did you have better things to report on, secrets to expose?"

"Exposing secrets isn't my thing." He closed the door and folded his arms against the bottom of the window frame. "My grandfather wanted me at a few management meetings. He still isn't back full-strength from his cancer treatments."

"So you backed him up?"

"I've always got his back." He pushed the door and circled around the truck, walking fast and easy. Behind her Oscar panted, watching vigilantly to make sure his master wasn't getting away. The driver side door popped open and Liam dropped behind the steering wheel. "When my parents were going at it, fighting like cats and dogs and I couldn't take it anymore, Pop was there. Every time I called him, every time I walked home from school to his house instead of mine, he answered. He took me in. I owe him."

"And you don't miss that exciting career you used to have?" She reached for her seat belt. "Wasn't it hard to give up?"

"Sure it was. I loved what I did, but I love my family more." His answer came simply, the most honest thing she'd ever heard. He bowed his head, plugging his key into the ignition, turning over the engine. "Pop's been a widower for most of my life. I'm his only grandson, and he had no one else. My dad is too wrapped up in his career, so no way could I let Pop down. I moved here because I wanted to make the most of the time we have left together, however long that is."

"That must be nice to be so close to him."

"It is." He maneuvered the truck out of the lot. He leaned in toward her, making the whole world tip at an angle.

Why was her reaction to him getting worse? Good thing she was sitting down because her knees turned to complete and total jelly. And breathing? Forget it. She couldn't draw in a single oxygen atom.

"I wouldn't trade Pop for the world."

The truth about Liam? Tough and masculine on the outside, a softie on the inside. And what did that do to the guards around her heart? They began to buckle again.

Danger. She didn't want to feel this way for any man, especially Liam. He was heartache waiting to happen. It was a good thing she had that interview, a blessing she had a reason to leave town.

Oscar poked his nose over the seat back and swiped a kiss against her cheek. The perfect distraction. She twisted to rub his head and gaze into those sweet doggy eyes. But she couldn't ignore the man capably driving, hands on the wheel, confident and at ease. Impossible not to notice the striking structure of his face—high slashing cheekbones, firm, strong jaw. All character.

Why did her stomach flutter?

A new thought suddenly occurred to her. Maybe Oscar's adorableness was getting past her defenses, and this wasn't Liam at all.

A girl could only hope.

"No, Oscar. Heel." Brooke did her best to sound authoritative, but it was tough to do when she was laughing so hard.

"This is never gonna work." The leash he held in both hands pulled tight until even the nylon stretched. "The stitching is going to hold, isn't it?"

"If not, we're in big trouble." The dappled shade tumbled over him, shifting golden bits into the dark sheen of his thick hair, onto the curve of his jaw, along the breadth of his chest. Laugh lines creased his face so attractively that they could make every woman in a ten-mile radius swoon.

Not her, she wasn't swooning. As long as she didn't look at him one second longer. She jerked away, focused on Oscar and grabbed his leash just above his collar. The dog stood on his hind legs, front paws planted solidly against a picket fence, watching little kids splash in a play pool, his tail whipping.

"Don't even think about jumping over," she warned him. "Oscar, down."

The Lab glanced over at her. Brows arched above innocent eyes as if to say, "What? I wasn't thinkin' that. Honest."

Yeah, right.

"Do you know what your problem is? You're too friendly." Lovingly she scrubbed the dog's head. "Down, boy."

Reluctantly his paws left the fence. He plopped to the sidewalk with a sigh.

"Heel." Liam tugged the leash gently. "C'mon, boy."

Oscar's head swiveled. He sniffed the air. He barked loudly and took off at a dead run. Liam dug in his heels. "Whoa. This isn't the Iditarod."

"I think he smells your neighbor's barbecue." Brooke dazzled as she jogged to keep up with the Lab. Laughing, hair blowing, moving with grace and ease. Open-hearted, happy, luminous, she turned around, moving backward. "There is something seriously wrong with your dog."

"Don't I know it. He just ate. Two entire pieces of pizza and three crusts."

"Don't forget the cheesy sticks he stole before we could catch him."

"At least he makes life an adventure." The physical adventures were the easiest kinds. Hopping on a plane, buckling in and zipping off to parts unknown. Landing in the Sudan, the Middle East, Somalia and never knowing what to expect. Each tragedy he covered, every struggle and war showed him another piece of the world. His team would set up a satellite feed and do a job. Then back on another plane. He never had time to get attached, to sink in and to commit.

But the emotional kinds of adventures? He was learning those were the toughest. He ran to keep up with the dog. "At least we know he'd make a good running buddy."

"If he actually kept running." Amused, Brooke swung away, dark hair curtaining her face as Oscar abruptly put on the brakes, skidding to a stop at the neighbor's lawn. With a whine, nose in the air, he pulled harder at his leash, frustrated when Brooke grabbed his collar.

"C'mon, boy. Heel." She earned an adoring look from the dog but his love of hamburgers was too strong. He lunged toward the neighbor's yard and her grip didn't loosen. "Sit." Firm, she pointed to the sidewalk beside her. "Oscar, sit."

Amazingly the dog's lunge fizzled. All four paws returned to the sidewalk. Oscar whined, struggling between the tantalizing aroma of charcoal burgers and pleasing the woman he obviously adored. Finally Oscar's doggy behind attempted to touch the ground, his decision made. He stared up adoringly at Brooke.

Couldn't blame the dog there. "Wow, I can't believe it. He's almost under control."

"All the way down, Oscar. C'mon." She pulled a treat out of her pocket. When the dog lunged for it, she whipped it away. "No. Sit. Sit and stay."

The Lab's ears sank. His head drooped. A whine squeaked out of his throat. The dog, obviously disappointed in himself, slunk into a sit, devastated at not being able to please.

"There. That's right. Good, good boy. I knew you could do it." She hunkered down beside the dog to hand over his treat. She rubbed his ears, kissed his nose and loved him up real good. Could he look away? Not a chance. Her gentleness hooked him like a fish on a line, reeling him in.

Don't fall for her, Liam. Be smart. Hold back. Remember the devastation a woman can do to a man's heart.

"Doggy!" A little girl toddled into sight next door, dripping water off her skirted swimming suit. She'd obviously been playing in a kiddy pool somewhere in the backyard. Her pigtails bobbed as she waddled across the lawn.

"It's Oscar!" A preschool boy dashed to catch up to her, water streaming down his face. He scrubbed it away with both hands as he ran closer.

"Hey, you two." At the sight of the neighbor kids, he got a good hold on Oscar's collar. "Looks like you've been playing in your pool again."

"Yep!" Nicholas skidded to a stop in front of Oscar. "My dad's makin' burgers."

"So I can smell." His hand bumped against Brooke's. They held the nylon strap together, fingers touching. Tenderness lodged somewhere behind his ribs with enough force that it was hard to ignore. The kids toddled closer. Oscar went wild, leaping and whining, so excited to see them again.

He really was a very good dog. Hard not to love the guy. Warmth seeped into his heart. And not only for the Lab. Brooke held him breathless as she greeted the little kids. Every shield seemed to tumble down, leaving her exposed. Sweet heart, kind spirit, gentle soul.

Impossible not to fall for that.

"He kissed me—he likes me!" The little boy beamed.

"Pretty doggy." Rosie held out one chubby hand and laughed when Oscar licked it. She scrunched her face up as the dog landed a kiss on her chin. She giggled happily.

"Hi, Liam," a woman's voice called behind the screen door. "How's the training going?"

"Hi, Marin. I think we're making progress."

"I suppose that's subjective." Marin laughed, squinting through the screen. "Is that Colbie with you?"

"No, it's Brooke."

"That's right. The missing sister. Hi, Brooke, good to meet you. Nicholas, bring your sister. The hamburgers are done. Supper time."

"Okay, gotta go, Oscar." Nicholas patted the dog's head one last time and seized his sister's hand. "C'mon, Rosie."

"No!" The little girl dug in her heels, eyes locked with Oscar's, but her brother tugged her along. She watched over her shoulder with big brown loving eyes.

Oscar whined, he cried, he lunged and finally hung his head when the kids disappeared behind the screen door.

"Poor guy. Do you know the trouble with you?" Brooke stroked his ears. "You are all heart."

Yes, Liam thought, that was exactly the part he was losing. His heart. Nothing could slow it down. Nothing held it back. He released his grip on Oscar's collar and straightened, gazing down at the woman, the real Brooke. She was all heart, too.

You're going to get hurt, buddy. That's what love does to a man.

But did his emotions listen to reason? Not a chance.

Chapter Twelve

Oscar trotted neatly behind her the short length of sidewalk heading toward his yard, panting. The Lab watched her intently, trying so hard to please. When a squirrel darted down a tree and streaked across the lawn, he lost all self-control. He yipped and lunged.

Good thing she'd shortened the leash and planted her feet.

"Sorry, but no. You can't even chase a squirrel when you're on a leash," she told him.

The dog huffed out a breath of air, seeming to understand her perfectly. Hard to resist the sweetie and his big brown eyes, but she neatly avoided meeting Liam's as her unsteady legs carried her down the walkway. The bungalow towered above them, bathed in dappled shade.

"Do you think he'll be ready to go jogging to-morrow?" Liam quipped as he pulled his house keys out of his jeans pocket.

"Sure, if you don't mind tripping over him." She felt as bright as the glancing rays of the sun slanting through the trees and as free as the wind rustling through the leaves. It had been a long time since she'd felt this happy. Weightless, as if she were floating. She followed Oscar and Liam into the cozy bungalow. "Although in the early morning there might be less distractions for him, so there could be less tripping."

"I'm ready to take the chance." He shut the door, dropped his keys on a little table and speared her with his luxurious blue gaze. Humor enriched the color, showing the man. "What's a few trips and tumbles? A couple of scraped knees? I'm tough. I can take it. As long as you come with us."

"Me? Run?" No. Absolutely not. All she could see was huffing and puffing behind him, dying of exertion. "It's been years since I've run. Nearly a decade."

"What's so hard about it? If you can walk, you can run." He unhooked Oscar's leash. "You want Brooke to come, right, buddy?"

"Ruff!" Oscar's bark echoed off the walls as he loped away, toe nails tapping on the hardwood.

"Like I can disappoint him now?" She shook her head. She used to love running. Being out on the open road with the peaceful Montana countryside rolling slowly by. Feeling strong in the zone, music humming through her headphones. The remembered freedom pulled at her now. "Fine, you've maneuvered me into it. I used to love to run."

"High school track?"

"Cross-country." She didn't mention the championships, the state record or the partial athletic scholarship she'd turned down because it hadn't been enough for her to afford college. But to run again? It's something she hadn't wanted to do in the city's dicier neighborhoods, dodging traffic and gangs. The more she thought about it, the more the idea grew on her. If she wasn't embarrassed by how out of shape she was.

"I ran cross-country, too. It kept me out of trouble." He led the way through the living and dining room to the kitchen. "I had some speed, which came in handy dodging bullets in Iraq."

"Or keeping up with Oscar racing down the sidewalk."

"True. A skill that's good, foreign or domestic."

The dog didn't bother to look up as they joined him in the kitchen. He lapped water from his water dish fast and hard. Her phone chimed a merry tune, surprising her. Her family knew she was with Oscar, so who could it be?

"Go ahead and get that." Liam yanked open the fridge door. "I've got root beer or grape soda."

"Grape, please." She squinted at her screen, not recognizing the name. The number looked local so she answered it. "Hello?"

"Is this Brooke?" a woman's voice asked. "The Dillards gave me your number. My name is Kerry Linton. I hear you train dogs."

"I attempt to." Looking at Oscar, she wasn't exactly sure how well she'd succeeded. "I'm not a professional or anything."

"I inherited my grandmother's beagle when she passed away and I can't get him to stop tinkling in the house. Do you think you can help?"

"I can give it a try." She couldn't believe she had another temporary job. Across the kitchen, Liam gave her a thumbs-up. She had a sneaking suspicion why the Dillards had recommended her. While he popped two can tops and opened the back door for the dog, she set a time during the weekend to meet Mrs. Linton.

"Word is getting around." Liam propped the screen door open. "Pretty soon you'll be so popular you won't be able to fit Oscar into your schedule."

"Oscar will always have the best spot in my schedule. At least for as long as I'm in town." She accepted the can he held out to her, nice and cold. She concentrated on the can and not the man in front of her.

Fine, so she could admit it. She didn't have the strength of will to look away from him. Who could? He was the kind of man determined to do what was right, who was kind to everyone, who'd given a dog on death row a new life. It wasn't a surprise tender emotions were creeping into her heart.

It was impossible for them to become anything more.

"You did this, didn't you?" She tried to speak past those tender emotions she couldn't get rid of. She took a little sip of soda, casual and determined to stay that way.

"I didn't do anything. Don't know what you're talking about." Dimples framed his dashing smile as he lifted his can.

"You told the Dillards." She glanced over her shoulder to see Oscar chasing a fluffy gray cat across his yard. "You didn't ask them to recommend me, did you?"

"Nope. I just said I'd hired you to train him, that's all." He followed her gaze. The feline leaped onto the top of the wooden fence and flicked his tail, glaring down at the dog with a superior look. "That cat has been teasing Oscar all week."

"And poor Oscar just wants to be friends."

"Exactly." For a moment their gazes met and the impact rolled through her like nothing she'd known before, rattling her heart, moving through her spirit and leaving her dazed.

Don't fall for him, she told herself. *Don't you do it.* She tried to summon up all the reasons why not, but her mind went blank.

That could not be a good sign. "Hey, can I ask

you a favor?" He leaned in, so close she could smell the soap on his skin and the fabric softener on his clothes.

"Sorry, all out of favors." The emotion within her flared, taking on a life of its own. Maybe she should escape while she still could.

"I need you to read my article for the Sunday edition." He forged ahead, shoes squeaking on the tile, drawing her along in his wake. "I want to know what you have to say. Your opinion matters to me."

"This is about the trial?" She swallowed hard, torn by the sight of the front door as they rounded the dining room table. Her pulse cannoned through her with enough force to rattle her ribs. She thought of her prison record. She thought of the chances Liam might see her and not the crime, like most people in her past had.

"Will you read it?" Sparkles glinted in Liam's true-blue eyes. Not the dashing flash of a man used to charming his way through the world, but the genuine glint of integrity that was hard to resist.

No. That was her decision. But what came across her lips? "Yes."

What hold did this man have on her? She followed him into his home office, set up in the spare bedroom. A few framed snapshots hung on walls and marched along the far corner of the desk. Pictures of combat troops, Afghan farmers, bone-thin children huddled in front of a Red Cross tent.

Liam, the reporter, wasn't a sensationalist feeding on other people's tragedies but a witness reporting them. Trying to bring light to human suffering. Her hands shook, wondering what was on the laptop screen he turned and nudged her way.

"Go ahead and sit." The chair wheeled closer. She felt his hands curl around her shoulders from behind, nudging her into the cushioned seat.

The words on the screen pulled her in, transporting her to Monday's courtroom under the glare of the fluorescent lights and the echoing rustles in the high-ceilinged room. The stoic jurors. The sorrow lingering in the air from the families who'd buried loved ones. A daughter, a brother, a father. All gone.

As she read, his words evoked the bang of the judge's gavel. The rumbling timbre of the district attorney's opening arguments. The muffled sobbing of Juanita's parents unable to hold back grief. The gruesome crime scene photos, bloody and heartrending and, later, the hostess's trembling narrative of watching her coworker fall to the ground, shot, limp as a rag doll.

Brooke set the soda can on the desk, forgetting to breathe. She leaned forward and scrolled down the document. Unable to take her eyes from the article, she kept reading, feeling his closeness and his unspoken question. When she reached the end of what he'd written, she cleared her voice.

"It's good." Her words still came out scratchy. "This is about the families. What they went through. What they lost."

"The rest of the article is all about the first person to fall. The busboy who tried to stop them." Liam knelt down beside her, larger than life. "I wanted to honor his courage and his life. I'm waiting until after Bree's testimony to write about Juanita. She has some memories I'd like to include, when she's ready."

The glowing softness gathering behind her sternum took on power. Emotions overwhelmed her. This wasn't tenderness and it wasn't affection, she stubbornly told herself. "You're not writing about the day-to-day progress of the trial?"

"That's Roger's job. I'm writing about the lives that are forever changed. That's what violence and injustice do." He covered her hand with his. As if their spirits touched, she felt the snap of connection in her soul. "That's what I write about. That's who I am."

"So I see." His words curled around her heart, warm with understanding. Eternity passed in a single moment. The world stopped spinning, time stood still and her fears vanished. For one perfect second the past evaporated and her feelings shone true.

I do adore him, she realized. With every breath, every beat of her heart and the infinite breadth of her soul.

"So, was that a yes on running tomorrow?" He opened his front door for her and watched the restless Montana breeze scatter silken tendrils across her forehead. Not easy to keep the caring he felt under control and hidden. When he wanted to reach out and brush fine strands of hair out of her eyes, he held back.

"How early?" She swiped the flyaway strands herself with a cute little sweep of her slender fingers. "I'm a morning person, but it's got to be within reason."

"How's six?"

"Doable. Did I thank you for recommending me to the Dillards?" She swirled out the door, pure grace and beauty. Why couldn't he stop noticing?

"You're welcome. I was just being honest." He glanced over his shoulder to check on Oscar, sound asleep on his dog bed, and left the door open. He followed her into the pleasant evening where mellow golden light played in the broad leaves of the maple trees. Birds twittered and the calls of children playing down the street added to the ambiance as he trailed down the steps after her. "You've helped more than you know."

"I guess we'll see come morning. Oscar has a

short attention span." She slowed her pace, waiting for him to catch up with her. "I think he'll be a great running buddy given a little time."

"He's already a great buddy." He fell into stride beside her and nothing had ever felt so right. Peace filled him, as resplendent as the evening. He prayed God was walking with him because love was a minefield. At least he knew Brooke was nothing like Sidney. "I wouldn't have taken Oscar back to the pound. Even if he and I had had a much more difficult transition time. You know that, right?"

"I do. That was my main reason for taking this job. My worry for him. After seeing how he'd strewn things around your house." She shook her head, laughed softly. Amazing.

His entire soul resonated. "And now?"

"I'm sort of fond of Oscar." Veiled, she spun away to dig keys out of her pocket. She made a lovely picture with gossamer strands framing her face, willowy and dainty. So lovely it made his eyes ache.

He couldn't read her. He just couldn't tell if she was in the same boat—with her feelings running away from her and not knowing what to do about it. How did you ignore the panicky feeling hitting like a tornado? Keep the faith and keep on going?

"I'm sweet on Oscar, too." He wasn't talking about the dog and he wasn't just fond of Brooke.

He took her keys from her and unlocked the truck door.

"Why do I feel watched?" She glanced around, squinting in the hazy light. "Oh, I know. Your neighbor is peering at us from her kitchen window."

"Marin's nosy." He opened the little pickup's door and leaned against it, watching Brooke over the door frame. He could not get enough of looking at her, just drawing her in. "She's an associate pastor at the church."

"That's why she knew Colbie. Colbie's so popular, she knows everyone. She gets around." She hesitated, gazing at him through the window she'd left open.

"Marin runs a lot of the senior programs. Gram adores her." He lifted a hand in a single wave, just to let Marin know he knew what she was up to. He could see a phone held to her ear. Apparently she had no shame because she waved cheerfully back.

"I have a terrible feeling she's talking with my grandmother. Gram assists with the seniors' Sunday school class every week." He shook his head, imagining the worse. "If she knew I was spending so much time with you, I'd never hear the end of it."

"Hey, join the club. You think this has been easy for me?" Amusement brought out the violet glints in her irises. Did she know what she did to him? "I've been taking heat all week from Lil and Colbie. Even Luke mentioned it. Don't expect any sympathy from me."

The quirk of a smile in the corners of her mouth said otherwise.

"It just proves you don't know my grandmother." His spirit brightened as he leaned in closer until it felt as if nothing separated them. "Since Grandpa Jim died, she has had a lot of time on her hands. Sure, she gardens more. Spends more time participating at church. But it's not enough. She still has plenty left over to devote to me."

"You're suffering because of it." Crinkles crept into the corners of her eyes. "It's tough being loved."

"Exactly. Glad you understand. Gram's gotten nosy, too."

"Funny, that's a common syndrome in my family."

They chuckled together and it felt good. *Right.* Like all the pieces of a puzzle fitting together, making a jumble finally clear. He could see evenings spent in her company, hearing her laughter, sharing moments where he felt relaxed, at peace, content. Whatever happened to the no trespassing sign on his heart? It had tumbled down long ago, was nothing but splinters now.

A howl shattered the stillness and radiated from the house with a force of an air raid siren. Doggy toenails scrabbled on hardwood, tapping counterpoint to the heartbroken yowling that increased in volume with every step. The yellow Lab rocketed down the step, cried out in relief and raced straight through the yard with the speed of a runaway motorcycle.

Goofy dog. Affection warmed him for this new addition to his life. Liam barely had time to brace himself before two paws hit his shoulders. Relieved brown eyes searched his and a pink lolling tongue swiped a kiss to his chin.

"It's okay, buddy." He rubbed the dog's head. "Did you wake up and find yourself alone?"

Oscar licked harder, whining deep in his throat, a high worried sound. Answer enough.

Fine, so his plan hadn't been to fall in love with the dog, either. "Everything's fine, boy. I didn't leave you. You can get down. Take it easy. That's right."

The big Lab dropped reluctantly to the ground, doggy brows pinched with worry, panting nervously. His poignant eyes found Brooke's and sadness tugged up his eyebrows. He whined again, a thin and nervous sound.

"Sorry, handsome, but I've got to go home." She knelt to rub the dog's soft head, besotted. Who wouldn't be? "But I'll be here tomorrow morning. Are you going to be a good boy while I'm gone?"

A doggy tongue shot out to swipe her chin. Perhaps that meant yes.

"You're going to remember how to sit and stay and heel, right?" She laughed at the second swipe of his tongue. "You are such an optimist, Oscar."

"One of us has to be," Liam quipped. Wonderful, compassionate Liam.

How did she hold back the tides of her heart? She had no clue. Overwhelmed, she swallowed hard, gave Oscar a final pat and rose full height. "Then I'll be optimistic, too. Tomorrow he's going to do fabulously. He won't chase one squirrel, right, Oscar? Not one kitty. Not one dog."

"Woof!" Oscar's head popped up, his eyes sharpened and he glanced eagerly around. Perhaps looking for a squirrel or a kitty or a dog. Funny guy.

"I'm taking that as an affirmative." She eased onto the truck's seat, reluctant. She didn't want to go. Worse, she couldn't even try to hide the truth from herself and blame it on Oscar. It was Liam she wanted to stay with. Liam she wanted to spend time with.

But it was time to go. No sense in prolonging the moment. Her future wasn't here in Montana. It could not be with him. Not Mr. Perfect. She remembered his story about Sidney and lost the ability to breathe. No doubt about it, he would only break her heart.

"Looks like your neighbor is still peeping at us." She plugged the key into the ignition.

"Marin isn't just peeping—she's reporting it to

whoever she's talking to on the phone." He worked her seat belt free and gave it a tug for her.

"As long as Colbie doesn't find out, that's all I care about." Amused, she fell silent when he leaned in to help her buckle it.

"Whatever Gram knows, she'll tell Lil. You know how they are." A thump hit the inside of his ribs so hard he had to wonder if his heart had survived intact. The wind blew flyaway strands of her hair against his neck. His hand trembled as he clicked the buckle into place. It took all his might to act casual. "We can't avoid those two. Best to head it off with a good offense."

"What do you meant?"

"Right after you leave I'm calling Gram." He straightened, reluctant to move away from her, to let this evening end. "Tell her all about the progress you're making with Oscar. I'll go on and on about the dog's training. It will disappoint her for sure."

"This might be the only time disappointing your grandmother is a good thing."

"Desperate times call for desperate measures."

"Then I'll do it, too." With a flick of her wrist, the engine puttered to life. "I'll lay it on thick for Colbie and Lil about how great Oscar is doing and it won't be much longer and the job will be done."

"I guess I hadn't thought that far ahead." He swallowed hard, fighting against feelings he wasn't ready for. Did she feel the way he did? Did she care for him, too? "Guess I thought you'd be here for a while. You've given me good advice, and look at Oscar."

"He's sitting!" Brooke softly brightened. "What a good boy."

He liked this side of her best, unguarded and open. Longing rushed through him, a yearning of the spirit so sweet he'd never known anything like it before. Pure and untarnished, complete feeling. He didn't want it, he wasn't ready for it, but it came all the same like dawn to the darkest night, like grace sifting into his life.

Oscar's tail thump, thump, thumped against the blacktop. So excited at his accomplishment, he bolted onto all fours and pranced around, dancing happily, panting, eyes shining with pride.

"Well, it was a start." Brooke shrugged, put the truck in gear and eased away from the curb. "Good night, you two. Be a good boy, Oscar."

Oscar's answering bark resounded along the street as the sun slipped below the horizon. Sepia light gilded the street, gilded her in the brief moment before he lost sight of the driver's side window. Her truck motored down the street and into the blaze of crimson and purple coloring the horizon. Something kept his emotions from retreating. A connection tied them, one he couldn't deny.

He thought he knew why, even when the truck puttered out of sight.

Is this You leading me, Lord? The breeze rip-
pled against the back of his neck, the reassurance
he needed.

Chapter Thirteen

The borrowed little pickup sputtered, idling roughly as she turned into the neighborhood's entrance and slowed for the speed bump. Folks were still out in the hazy twilight following sunset. A trio of grade school kids on bikes pedaled up the street, a little white dog yapping at their heels. An elderly couple waved as she went by on the last leg of their evening walk. A few neighbors sat on their porch swings while others gave thirsty flower beds a good watering. Everybody she passed lifted a hand in greeting.

It gave her a cozy feeling. Much different than living in a big city. She pulled off the lane, tires crunching in the strip of gravel bordering Lil's lawn. Newly mowed, she noticed. Luke or Hunter must have done it before they returned to their farm for the night. Her phone chimed announcing a text just as she flicked the key and the engine died. She dug out her cell, eager to read the message. Of course it was from Liam.

I totally threw Gram off. Not hard to imagine the flash of his dimples as he'd written that. I went on about what a great dog trainer you were. Genius dog whisperer, I called you.

Wow. I could get a reality show with that title. She hit Send and clicked free of the seat belt.

That's what Gram said. His message marched across her screen. Easy to imagine humor warming the tone of his words. Easier to remember how his good-hearted humor dazzled her. Against her will, he was winning her heart.

Her phone chimed again. She opened the door, stepped into the evening and read his next message. Just wanted to let you know going on the offensive worked.

That you know of. She couldn't resist a little more humor.

What does that mean? His question came back to her.

As I type this, someone is peering at me from behind her living room sheers. She stopped to give Madge a finger wave.

Don't leap to conclusions, his next text advised. She may be thinking what a good dog trainer you are.

Or wondering how to package me to network

bigwigs. She closed the truck door with her elbow and crunched through the gravel.

If she is, do I get a cut?

Why not? She tapped out as she walked through the grass. It's the least I can do. Oops, gotta go.

"Brooke?" Liam's grandmother stared at her from the edge of the privacy fence. "Is it true what I hear?"

"That depends on what you've heard." She ambled closer. "Your grandson exaggerated about the dog whisperer thing. I'm not a real dog trainer."

"You have a natural knack, then. You made a difference in that dog's behavior. Liam's not exaggerating about that." Sprightly blue eyes appraised her. "Marin and I got to talking and I'm thinking you should put up a flyer on the church bulletin board. Let folks know you help with problem cases."

"That's a good suggestion. It's nice of you to think of me, but I'll be leaving at the end of Bree's trial."

"You never know, dear. You may have to change your plans. You always have to be open to what God has in store for you. Your family needs you here. Surely you can see that." Madge tugged on her garden gloves and reached for her watering hose. "I've seen all you've done to help Colbie. Taking out the garbage, watering the lawn, seeing to Lil's care."

"I've just done a few things." She shrugged. "How did you notice all of that?"

"Just call me nosy." Madge gave the nozzle a twist and water sprinkled out, raining on her border roses.

Nosy? More like a neighbor who cared.

"Good night," she called, heading across the lawn and up the steps. The minute she opened the door she smelled popcorn. Pops and bangs echoed inside the kettle as Colbie stood at the stove, giving it a good shake.

"You arrived just in time for popcorn, dear." Delighted, Lil wheeled out of the kitchen. "My, but you look happy. Did you have fun tonight?"

"With that dog around it's impossible not to." She dropped the keys on the entry table. "Where's everyone else? I still have Bree's truck."

"She said to keep it. She and Brandi rode home together. Max said he wouldn't mind giving her a ride when she needed it. He's so good to her. I'm thankful she found him." Lil sighed with motherly joy. "Your brothers headed home to check on the cows. Colbie and I are just about to sit down and watch a reality show. We're going to see which model gets sent home tonight."

"How about I get the drinks and join you in the living room?"

"That's sweet of you, especially since I've helped Colbie all I can."

"Then I'll take over."

With a smile Lil zipped away in her electric chair, chugging toward her spot by the couch.

"Did I hear you agree to help me?" Colbie asked over the symphony of popping going on in the kettle. "I'd be happy to put you to work."

"Awesome. You look like a woman in need of a bowl."

"Desperately. Usually I think ahead, but I was distracted by the twins leaving." Colbie gave the kettle a last jiggle over the burner. "You seem pretty bubbly. All pink and glowing."

"It's the sun. I'm not used to it living in Seattle."

"Are you sure it's from the weather?" The pops began slowing down so Colbie shut off the stove and sidled up to the bowls. "Maybe all that glow is from being with a certain someone?"

Honestly. "Fine. I confess it. I'm sweet on a certain someone."

"Ooh! I knew it!" Triumph accentuated Colbie's words as fluffy white corn tumbled into a blue plastic bowl. "Liam."

"No. It's Oscar."

"The dog? Oh, that's not what I wanted to hear."

"Really, how could I resist? Those big brown eyes. That blond glossy hair. He had me at woof."

"Funny. But now I'm disappointed. With Bree and Max engaged, I'm getting optimistic. Since Bree has found her happily-ever-after, the rest of you can, too." Colbie upended the kettle and gave it a shake. The last fluffs tumbled into the bowl, fragrantly delicious.

"Hey, don't look at me." She took three cans of soda from the fridge and plunked them onto the counter. "I don't have to guess how any man is going to react when he learns about my history. I've seen it up close and personal. At church, at Bible study and even at the animal shelter."

"Oh, surely not every guy."

"Whenever a nice guy would get that look in his eye like he wanted to get to know me better or ask me out, all I had to do was to tell him I'd served time. Off he went, avoiding me from that moment on like I was infected with Ebola."

"Brooke, I didn't know." Colbie set the kettle on a cold burner with a clunk. "Here I've been trying to fix you up."

"So, you admit it." She pulled three squares from the paper towel roll. "Finally!"

"I want you to be happy. It wasn't fair that you lost all those years in prison when it wasn't your fault."

"You don't have to fix everything, Colbie."

"I know. I get in the habit of taking care of Mom and I can't seem to stop myself." She poured a drizzle of melted butter over each mound of popcorn. "Liam could be different. He's seen a lot of the world. He's honorable. He would understand."

I doubt it. The words died on her lips. One look at the quiet hope in Colbie's violet eyes and she couldn't do it. She knew Colbie was wrong, but how could she fault her sister for wanting the best for her? So instead of arguing she grabbed bowls of corn, cans of sodas and napkins and kept her feelings buried. She didn't want to admit it but tonight with Liam had changed her. Nothing was the same. Not her mood, not her thoughts and not her outlook.

Deep down inside grew the tiniest seed of hope. That somewhere a good man would understand. That she had a chance for a close, wonderful relationship that felt like it had tonight. That she had a chance for happiness and a happily-ever-after.

Don't picture Liam, she told herself but it was too late. His chiseled good looks, muscled strength and kindness filled her thoughts. Emotion surged through her like a summer sun, chasing away shadows and darkness.

She had to be practical. Even as compassionate as Liam was, chances still weren't good he would understand. He would think she was like Sidney, keeping the unsavory parts of her past from him, letting him see only the good. Besides, next week she would be gone. With God's will her interview would go well and she would be building a life in Portland.

Liam? He was never meant to be hers. Somehow she had to find a way to get past caring for the man. Even if it hurt.

"Oh, that popcorn smells so good." Lil's cheer filled the living room.

She wasn't in love with Liam, she told herself stubbornly as she set Lil's drink within easy reach. This was a crush, something she could get over. It absolutely, positively wasn't love. She wouldn't let it be.

Morning light flooded his room as Liam woke with a start. He blinked at the tumble of cheerful sun cutting around the blinds. A deep, soft snoring rumbled from the foot of his bed where a big yellow dog lay, sprawled out, legs every which way.

Funny guy. Oscar had crept into his heart. Liam reached over to hit the alarm clock off before it buzzed. Too late. The buzzer pierced, and Oscar woke with a start and bounded onto all fours, rocking the mattress. Oscar flew off the bed and dashed across the room and down the hall. An excited bark echoed through the house as if to say, "Oh, boy, another great day!"

There was nothing like having a dog, Liam decided as he pulled on his jogging clothes, shuffled into a pair of running shoes and bumbled down the hall, half asleep. Oscar hopped excitedly at the back door. The minute it opened, Oscar hurdled across the deck. The neighbor's fluffy gray cat sat on the top of the fence, tail curling.

The dog had it right. It was a great day. Feeling as cheerful as the morning, Liam grabbed a clean cup from the top dishwasher rack. Automatic coffeemakers with timers were great blessings. He breathed in the bracing aroma of brewed coffee and the sweet May air breezing in through the door. Best of all, Brooke would be coming by this morning. His heart? It burned brighter than the sun thinking of her.

Time to admit the truth. He missed her presence, he missed her humor, he missed everything about her. He dug coffee creamer out of the fridge and poured steaming coffee into a cup. The minutes dragged by without her. He shook his head. Hard to believe how fast she'd come to mean so much to him. Here he was counting the seconds full of longing for the lovely sight of her face.

I'm trusting You, Lord. Knowing he wasn't alone, that God was in charge, he took his cup to the window. He had a good view as Oscar romped and stretched his legs in the backyard, running along the fence with canine enthusiasm. Now and then he would circle around to plead up at the cat. His whine seemed to say, "Let's be friends."

The cat delighted himself by hissing.

This dog was definitely livening up Liam's life. He took another bracing sip and let the comforting flavor roll across his tongue, waking him up. It was a few minutes before six, which meant Brooke would be here soon. His mind and his heart kept returning to her. Her quiet beauty, her gentleness and how she'd shone last night, all guards down. Vulnerable.

Just like he was. Love was a dangerous proposition. But she was nothing like Sidney. She wasn't holding back secrets and hiding parts of herself. She wasn't trying to use him to start a new life. Brooke was sweet and truthful and compassionate.

No way would gentle-hearted Brooke hurt anyone.

Something warm and wet lapped his hand. Oscar's tongue. "Hey, there, buddy. Are you done trying to charm the neighbor's cat?"

Oscar answered with a loud pant. His ears perked. His nose went up. He tilted his head, listening. When he broke into an excited doggy boogie and barked with great excitement, it could only mean one thing.

"It's six o'clock. Did you hear Brooke drive up?"

Another round of thrilled barking and doggy dancing.

"My sentiments exactly." He set down his coffee and locked the back door. Side by side, he and Oscar cut a path through the house comfortable together, best friends for keeps.

He opened the door before she could knock.

With her satin dark hair swept up in a messy ponytail, wearing a faded gray T-shirt and black athletic shorts, she took his breath away. A natural beauty.

With Brooke, what you saw was what you got. Wholesome. Honest.

Wow.

With an excited bark, the big Lab sprang, all four paws bouncing off the porch boards. Brooke stepped back, ever kind, gently firm. "Sit, Oscar."

Doggy brows furrowed as he slunk to all four paws. Valiantly wrestling for self-control, his haunches sank and rose, sank and rose. It was a great struggle, but finally his tail thumped on the porch floor, victorious. Ears pricked, head up, eyebrows quirked with surprise, he sat like the perfect dog he was.

"Good dog, Oscar! Yay!" She pulled a treat out of her pocket and handed it over. "Woo-hoo."

Oscar politely took the treat between his teeth, looking wildly impressed with himself. His ability to sit on command was no longer a onetime thing.

"Brilliant, Oscar." He scrubbed the dog's head and snapped on a leash. "Are you ready to run?"

Happily crunching, the Lab seemed to nod.

Every instinct Liam had shouted at him that this was his last chance. He was reaching the point of no return with Brooke, but he wasn't as panicked as he used to be. He locked the door, drank in the lovely picture Brooke made on his porch and let his feelings go. Love whispered through him like the sweet morning's breeze. "Ready to do it?"

"Let's go." With a flash of her smile and a whip of her ponytail, she dashed ahead of him down the walk. Lissome stride, athletic sureness, she held his attention as they spilled onto the sidewalk. Oscar raced ahead, darting after a squirrel scurrying up a tree.

"Heel, Oscar." He moved before Brooke did, shortening the leash, tugging the dog to his side as she'd taught him, praising Oscar for staying there. The Lab glowed, loping along, his happiness contagious.

"He's doing pretty well." Brooke sounded a little breathless, so he adjusted his pace to match her shorter one. She laughed when Oscar spotted a cat on a porch and yanked away. The same gray cat that had been teasing him on the fence. "Oops. I spoke too soon. Oscar." She snapped to get his attention.

"Heel, boy." He praised the dog when Oscar complied. "Hey, this is working."

"I think Oscar's starting to settle down, aren't you, boy?" Caring deepened the violet-blue tint of her irises, making them impossibly deep, incredibly kind. "And you. You've trained up pretty nicely, Liam."

"I'm proud of myself. I've made good progress."

"Yes, you have." She loped with a runner's easy stride, like someone born to do it. "Oscar just needed to get used to his new life. I can't imagine how worried he had to be at the animal shelter, wondering if anyone would want him. He had to be so excited when you chose him. Once he figures out that this is his life now and you won't let him down, that's all he needs."

This close to her, he felt her next step, her next breath, her next heartbeat. She was a whisper moving through his spirit. But did he move through hers? Or were his affections a one-sided deal?

"This is our last training session." She looked in the zone, arms relaxed, stride easy, shoes striking the pavement in a steady rhythm. Pink dotted her cheeks. Happiness polished her, made her incandescent. "You don't need me anymore."

"Need you? Sure, we need you." He had to stay vulnerable, he had to stay open and take a risky step not knowing if she was feeling the same. "Oscar still has some problems. Plus, he'd be bummed to lose you."

He wasn't only talking about Oscar.

"I'd be bummed to lose him, too." Maybe she wasn't only talking about Oscar, either. She blushed, looking down, and that flash of vulnerability gave him hope. Powerful affection cinched him up tight.

Please see what I can't say, he pleaded. *What I*

can't put into words. This was where he'd failed with Sidney. Always keeping to the surface, shying away from deeper feelings and the emotional openness that hurt like a wound. He'd never been open and vulnerable with Sidney. He wasn't making that mistake again.

"Look, he's limping." She twisted to get a better look at Oscar's gait. With the wind in her hair, she was beauty in motion. Her forehead crinkled. "It's not much, but he's definitely favoring his front leg."

"I see it." He slowed to a stop, concerned. "Maybe he pulled a muscle or something?"

"Maybe. Let me see." She huffed to a stop, out of breath, trying to ignore the stitch in her side. Oscar gazed up at her innocently, eyes wide, ears up, wondering why they'd stopped.

"What's sore, boy?" She knelt on rubbery legs. "Is it your paw?"

Oscar gladly lifted his paw, ready to shake. She cradled his hand in hers, gently checking for a thorn or perhaps a small pebble that might have gotten wedged between his pads. Nothing.

"His paw doesn't seem to be hurting him." She ignored the twist in her soul as Liam hunkered down beside her, breathing easily, hardly winded. She resisted the need to look at him because she had to keep this simple. She didn't want to get her hopes dashed. She was leaving next week. And even if she wasn't, a man like Liam would hardly want a felon for a wife.

"No, this feels okay, too. No heat, nothing swollen or tender. At least he's not whimpering." She gently palpated Oscar's ankle and inched her fingertips along the lean bones of his lower leg. He whimpered and jerked away, eager to put his paw back on the ground where it belonged.

"What—what's wrong?" Liam hand curled over the Lab's neck to soothe him.

"He's sore there, that's for sure." She rubbed the dog's head. "Maybe it is a pulled muscle, but you really should take him to a vet just to be safe."

"A vet. Do you know of a good one?"

"No, but I'm sure Oscar's day care can give a good recommendation."

"Great. You're handy to have around, Brooke McKaslin." He leaned in closer, intent, garnering her attention, impossible to look away from.

"I have my moments," she sputtered, trying to be casual, hoping to sound natural but air caught in her throat and she gasped, only once, embarrassingly overwhelmed by his nearness. By the warm gleam of blue and black in his eyes, by the manly texture of his unshaven jaw, by the deep unspoken hope she felt. A hope she didn't dare give voice to.

"Thanks for noticing his limp." His hand curled gently around hers; it was like he was holding on.

Like his touch said something more. "You should work in a vet's office. You'd be good at it."

"That's what I'd always wanted to do." Regret returned; it was always the cloud overhead, casting a shadow. That was her past. She wanted to erase it, to obliterate it forever. Because then she would be free to let the affection within her become something great and rare. Something she'd been dreaming of all her life. True love with a good man.

The morning light burnished him, catching the highlights in his hair, emphasizing the perfect cut of his shoulders. Exposing his heart.

He cared for her. He really cared. Never had a man gazed at her the way Liam did. Respect and devotion etched into the planes of his face, deepened the blue of his eyes and pulled her inescapably closer to him. She'd been alone for so long, longing to be loved, never daring to wish.

Lord, do I dare ask for this hope to come true?

Liam's gaze shifted downward to trace the curve of her lips. Her pulse galloped shakily as he leaned closer, his mouth hovering over hers, his eyes looking into her until they drifted shut and their lips met.

Definitely a wish come true. She gave herself up to the sweetness of his kiss, curled her fingers into his shirt and let his brightness fall over her. His kiss filled her with pure brilliance, perfect peace and a love so radiant she was blind to everything else.

When he lifted his lips from hers, the sun became dazzling. She let him gather her in his strong arms and fold her against his wide chest. She closed her eyes, breathed in the scent of fabric softener on his shirt, resting against him, leaning on him. Soul overflowing, the bond of their hearts remained.

"That went well," he quipped shakily, as if he was deeply affected, too.

"It did." They smiled together, snuggled beneath the fall of morning sun. Not one to be left out, Oscar leaned over to snuggle close and add a tongue swipe across her face.

"Oscar!" she protested, laughing. Happy? That wasn't the word. Joy filled her, pure enough to chase away every shadow of the past. Feeling like a whole new woman, as if her life could be full of possibilities, she wanted to hold on to this perfect moment forever.

Chapter Fourteen

The moment couldn't last forever. Eventually she had to move away from his sheltering arms. A car trundled down the residential street, probably someone leaving for work, breaking the moment. The laughter faded and so did the bliss of that wonderful hope. Gazing into Liam's flawless eyes, full of affection and character, she saw her wishes fall away. What would he think of her if he knew about her mistakes? About her drug charges?

Reality hit like a punch. She grimaced, took the pain and moved away from him, creating a physical distance. Oscar panted happily, searching both her and Liam for clues on what fun things they were going to do next. The morning had lost its luster as she flicked the end of her ponytail over her shoulder. That kiss shouldn't have happened. She never should have allowed it.

She'd never wanted anything more.

"Guess we should circle back. Probably walk." Liam reached for her hand. She let him, even when she knew she should pull away. He tightened his grip on Oscar's leash and set the pace, irresistibly amazing. The wish for him remained in her heart, stubbornly refusing to let go.

When had they made the step from friend to something more? Why hadn't she stopped it? She took a wobbly step, surprised to find her muscles shaky. Maybe because she knew she shouldn't be holding on to him. She didn't have the right. She wasn't what he thought. He didn't know her darkest moments.

"He seems to be okay walking, even loping a little." Liam tilted his head to study Oscar's prance. "No, I guess he's favoring that right leg barely."

"It's hardly noticeable, but it's there." She angled a bit to get a better look. "I wonder how long that's been going on?"

"No idea. I'll keep an eye on it. I'm sure the vet will need to know." He studied her out of the corner of his eye. "You should check into getting into a vet assistant program."

"I keep hearing this. Are you and Colbie in cahoots?"

"I admit it. She paid me to say that." He winked, obviously kidding. "No, honest. You might want to see what it would take."

"It's a nice thought. I feel like it's too late to

change the path I'm on." She sounded light and breezy, but he knew her heart.

"It's never too late for dreams." He hardly noticed the reason why Oscar gave a bark and raced over to sniff at a chain-link fence. Vaguely he heard another dog's answering bark and caught sight of a friendly canine smile on the other side of the fence. Brooke dominated his attention. Her unassuming elegance captured him. He couldn't help noticing she seemed shuttered again since their kiss.

What a kiss. He'd felt her affection in that kiss, the truth of her heart. Had she felt his?

"Dreams? I'd almost forgotten about those." She bit her bottom lip, a little wistful. The copper highlights in her hair gleamed in the sunlight.

"Maybe it's time to remember them." Fathomless tenderness reared up inside him as he tugged on Oscar's leash, bringing the dog to heel. When she smiled up at him, he felt ten feet tall. "Maybe I should, too."

"What does that mean? You help manage your grandfather's newspaper. You've traveled the world. Don't tell me you've run out of dreams."

"I did for a while. Then Oscar came along." *And you,* he wanted to say. A wave of tenderness rolled through him, filling him to the brim. What did she think about that kiss? Had she liked it? Wished it hadn't happened? Was that why she seemed farther away emotionally? She waltzed along, possessing his heart and she didn't even know it.

"You always dreamed of having a dog?" Even asking the question, she kept staring ahead watching the sidewalk, the dog, the car across the street back out of its driveway. Everything but him.

"It was all I wanted when I was a kid," he confessed. "A friendly dog who would be my best friend, who wouldn't leave me when my parents were fighting. They were at it a lot."

"Mine, too. I know how that feels." Soft and tender feelings left him helpless. He'd never been this vulnerable, laid wide open, defenseless. When she left for Oregon, she was going to shatter him.

He could try to cinch up his heart, anchor it good and protect himself as hard as possible. But the sunlight found her, drawing his gaze. The wind fluttered the flyaway tendrils framing her delicate face. Dreams he'd buried came back, brand-new and better than before. Images of Brooke in a white dress walking down the aisle, of her in his home, in his life, in his arms cradling their newborn.

All that he had seen in the world, the places he'd been, the people he'd met, he'd been smart enough to learn that the real things in life weren't fame or money, success or status. Love and family were the only things that mattered. Gentle, honest Brooke understood that, too. He didn't need to hear her say it to know it. He could feel it in the connection, in her smaller hand tucked into his. Knowing her had changed his life.

She had changed him. Given him back the illusions Sidney had taken from him. The belief that a woman's heart could be true enough to make love last.

The problem was she would be leaving. His Grandfather Knightly and Grandmother Jones were getting older. They needed him here. He had to stay. Where did that leave them?

"Honestly?" She broke the companionable silence, drawing him out of his thoughts. "I'm glad we're not jogging back. I'm seriously out of shape. It's embarrassing."

"Do you know what you need to do?"

"I couldn't guess."

"You should run more." It sounded like a good idea to him. "Since I'm not sure Oscar should be putting miles on that leg of his, I'm down a running buddy."

"You never had a running buddy since technically this is Oscar's first run." She arched a brow at him, not buying it.

"Right. But I was looking forward to having a running partner and now I'm disappointed."

"So sorry." She wasn't going to be charmed by him. Letting him kiss her had been crazy enough. "Life is full of disappointments."

"And you're saying this because…?" He quirked an eyebrow, dashing enough to take her breath away.

A smart girl would keep right on breathing. She had no business bantering with him. Or wanting what she could not have. Her chin went up, her spine steeled and she tried to find some of that willpower she used to have before she met him.

"Because I don't want to get into the habit of saying yes to you," she admitted. "You are a dangerous man."

"Me? No way." He shook his head, scattering thick shanks of hair, dimples flashing. "I'm as safe as they come."

"I beg to differ." Did he not remember the kiss? How could she ever forget it? The tenderness of his kiss lingered on her lips and in her heart. She wasn't entirely sure it would ever leave.

"I don't know what happened to you in your last relationship, but it was bad enough you haven't dated in a long, long time." His house came into sight and he let go of Oscar's leash. The dog pranced through the yard, turned around halfway up the walk and stared at them curiously. Liam didn't seem to notice. He zeroed in on her, intense blue eyes, manly appeal and tenderness. Irresistible.

"It's not easy for me to talk about." Now would be the time to tell him. To tell him about how far her trust and her life had been shattered, but the words caught in her throat and would not budge. And why? Because he would never look at her this way again. She didn't want this to end.

"That's all right, Brooke." His tone warmed over her name, ringing deep with affection.

Affection she could not turn away from as he angled in, cradled her chin in his hands and looked at her as if she were precious. She shouldn't allow this. She ought to step away, put distance between them and let him know she was not what he thought. But her feet didn't move, the words refused to come and she was left gazing up at him, captivated by his regard for her.

"You have nothing to worry about from me." He drew himself up taller, looking heroic like a storybook character come to life. "I would never hurt you. I would stand in front of a bullet to save you from it, from any pain."

She believed him. Impossible not to. She, who vowed never to trust a man, trusted him. He was too good to be true, honorable to the core and far too good for her.

Just tell him the truth, Brooke. He deserved to know. Gazing into his eyes, feeling like she'd met her perfect match, that in another time long ago, God had made them for each other. They were kindred souls meant to be together forever. The words stayed bunched in her throat.

She couldn't do it. She couldn't break the

moment. Once he knew, he wouldn't look at her like he cared.

He wouldn't want her. Maybe it was better to leave it like this. She would go on with her life and could always look back on this beautiful memory with him. But was that enough?

A cold pelt of water whirred across her, slapping against her back. Her mind was caught up in her dilemma so she wasn't thinking clearly when she spun around and got a face full of spray. The underground sprinkler had come to life, shooting sparkling jets through the sunny lawn and onto her. Oscar barked in glee, leaping to chase the offenders, and Liam chuckled. He eased in front of her to protect her from the worst of the stream.

"I forgot about the sprinkler." He laughed, rolled his eyes and looked adorable with droplets in his hair. "That's what I get for wondering if I should kiss you again."

"That's definitely a sign you should keep your lips to yourself." With Liam, it seemed like she was always laughing as she spun away. She pulled the pickup's keys from her pocket. "See ya, Oscar."

Oscar's cheerful "ruff!" echoed above the whizzing and spitting sprinkler heads.

"What, you aren't going to say goodbye to me?" Liam called after her. Wind tousled and water logged, he was more stunning than any one man had the right to be.

"I'm not at all sure what to do about you," she quipped, unlocked the door and dropped onto the seat. The rumbling peal of his laughter warmed her heart and soul as she drove away.

"Brooke?" Colbie spoke over the clatter in the kitchen, where she was making breakfast. "Did you want scrambled or fried?"

"Whatever's easiest." Brooke slipped her keys on the entry table. "Need some help?"

"I won't turn it down." Colbie poured a steaming cup of coffee—bless her—and slid the cheerful mug with a big smiley face onto the counter. Brooke followed the wondrous scent into the kitchen. Caffeine. Just what she needed to kickstart her brain. Maybe then she could think of something besides Liam.

"So, how's Liam?" Colbie sailed over to the fridge, where she grabbed a carton of eggs and a bottle of coffee creamer. She set both on the counter. "What? I saw that eye roll."

"I'm trying not to think of him." Of how marvelous his kiss was. How at peace she felt, whole and alive, when he'd taken her hand. How easy it was to laugh with him.

"I can't imagine why. If I were you and I had a great man like that wanting to date me, ooh." She cracked an egg and tipped it into the sizzling frying pan. "You couldn't pay me to stop thinking about him."

"You deserve a good man, Colbie. Someone to sweep you off your feet." She upended the coffee creamer over her cup, pulled out the silverware drawer and scooped up a spoon. "Someone really phenomenal."

"Me? I told you. Personally, I don't need an attractive, nice, well-off, phenomenal man." She cracked another egg and tossed the shell into the garbage.

"And I need one?" she quipped.

"I don't get why you're reluctant. If this is about what Darren did to you, you've got to let that go." Colbie chose another egg from the carton. "Don't let him rob any more of your life. Grab happiness with both hands. Don't let it go. Liam is such a good guy."

"I know." Wasn't that the problem? He was trustworthy. If he was any less wonderful, this situation would be so much easier. She could just let him go. Frustrated, she leaned against the counter, cradling the cup, breathing in coffee-scented steam. "If I tell him and he runs away as fast as he can go, I don't think I'll get over it."

Fear wrapped around her stomach with a cruel grip, squeezing tight.

"What if he understands?" Colbie lowered the burner heat, set down her spatula and breezed closer. "Maybe he can see the good in you the way the rest of us do."

"Oh, Colbie." Tears burned behind her eyes. She set down her cup before she spilled it and tried to breathe in, but hope blocked the way. Hope for love with Liam rose up with a strength she could no longer deny. All that she'd been fighting to hold back overwhelmed her. Colbie's arms wrapped around her with sisterly love. Brooke held on so tight.

Was there a chance he could understand?

"You're more lovable than you think." After a good hard comforting squeeze, Colbie eased away. "God loves you. We love you. Liam adores you."

"Adores? Isn't that a rather strong word?" She had nothing left. No denial, no steel, no defenses to protect her. She was more exposed and vulnerable than she wanted to be. Love she was afraid to feel soared through her like fluffy, flawless clouds in a perfect summer sky. All she could think about was his kiss. How he'd cradled her chin and gazed into her eyes. How she'd caught glimpses of a dream she'd thought long dead.

What if?

"Just talk to him. Tell him." Colbie retrieved her spatula and flipped an egg. "My guess? He'll understand. You can't let the past diminish your future. Isn't it worth the risk?"

Yes, her heart answered. *No,* her fears said.

"Just think about it." Colbie flipped another egg

and the front door squeaked open. The twins' conversation echoed in the little entryway. "Hey, you two."

"I'll go wake Lil and help get her dressed." Brooke pushed away from the counter. Time to get the day started. It was another big day ahead of them.

"No way, your breakfast is almost ready," Colbie said over the scrape of the spatula and the spit of frying eggs.

"Too bad. I'm doing it." She launched away from the counter. "Don't even think about arguing."

"Since when did you get so bossy?" Colbie tilted her head. "Does this mean you like it here? That you can't live without us?"

"I know what you're doing. I can't stay." She paused at the doorway, smiled at the twins and took in Colbie and her spatula. Her dear sisters. The bigger question might be how was she going to leave?

"Thanks for helping with Mom." All humor faded as Colbie lifted the pan from the stove. Gratitude shone in her blue-violet gaze.

"No problem. You're not alone, not while I'm here." Brooke turned on her heel. She could feel her sister's smile light up the morning.

Brooke. Liam couldn't concentrate on anything else as he ambled across the street. Not the ring of his cell phone. Not the familiar faces of his peers in the morning crowd rushing toward the courthouse. Not even the curb at his feet, which he almost tripped on.

Amazing, incredible and sweet Brooke, a woman he could believe in. She lit his life like the sun and moon combined. Only her face stood out in the swarm of folks, lovelier than all the rest. Certainty filled him as he gripped his laptop case, cut in front of a crew from the local TV station and arrowed in her direction.

"Liam!" she called, too far away to talk but the affection shining in her voice was answer enough. It felt like a prayer answered and he was grateful down to his soul.

She set the brake on Lil's wheelchair, her glossy dark hair tumbling forward to shield her face. A good twenty yards separated them, but the devotion he felt for her bridged any distance. The happiness of their morning run stuck with him—and that kiss. He shook his head. His heart thumped in his chest. Nothing on earth had been as pure as her kiss.

"It's Liam!" Colbie called, finally spotting him in the crowd. With the McKaslin family surrounding Lil's chair, he lost sight of Brooke for a moment. When she rose from kneeling, her long silky curtain shifted, revealing her smile.

One that matched his. He had it bad for her. Tenderness ebbed higher, threatening to overflow. Places in his spirit opened and gentled simply from looking at her. He had to ignore the fear of trusting another woman again because he didn't want to miss out on this chance with Brooke. She wasn't Sidney. She wasn't walking around with secrets to hide. He knew the real Brooke. He loved her.

Love. He shook his head. He never thought that would happen again. Somehow the wounded places in him had healed. Good thing the no trespassing sign had come down on his heart.

"Hi, stranger." Brooke waltzed forward to meet him and their gazes clashed as if God was bringing them together.

This time he wouldn't get hurt. This time a happily-ever-after was meant to be.

"Need any help?" He resisted the need to pull her close. He was bashful, his heart far too exposed. "I'm an excellent wheelchair pusher."

"Then we'll put you to work." She held out her hand and he enfolded it in his. Perfect fit.

"How's Bree doing?" He nodded toward the SUV where the brothers were taking charge of Colbie's keys and making sure Lil had everything she needed. "I heard it might be her day today."

"Maybe this afternoon. Depends on timing." Her stomach knotted in worry for her sister. She knew firsthand how difficult and intimidating it was to sit in that seat and relive the worst moments of your life.

"She looks good. Something tells me her family rallying around her doesn't hurt."

"Plus Max hasn't left her side." It meant everything to see how devoted Bree's fiancé was to her. It helped her believe that maybe there were more happy endings in this world than sad ones.

Hope. It lifted through her like grace. With Liam's fingers twined through hers it felt as if nothing could go wrong. Only blue skies ahead. As long as he understood when she told him the truth.

"Liam." A woman stepped out of the crowd to block their way. Her curly brown hair and heavy makeup seemed vaguely familiar. "Rumor has it your grandfather's back at work. Glad to hear it. Looks like you've got yourself an exclusive."

The reporter. The one who'd approached her in the courthouse. Brooke's jaw dropped. Ice shot through her veins. She watched in horror as the woman cut her cold eyes Brooke's way.

A chill fluttered through her, a warning of what was to come. She tried to pull Liam away but her feet froze to the ground. She couldn't move one muscle, not one, as panic drilled through her.

No. The only word that flashed in her mind. *No. No. No.*

"I'm doing a piece on recovery. With your drug

history, maybe you could give me an interview." A catlike smile crept across Tasha Brown's features. "It would tie in nicely with the trial. What do you say?"

Time stood still. The din of the crowd faded to silence. In the space between heartbeats her eyes met Liam's. She read the shock in his honest blue depths, the disbelief. This was the time to tell him the truth, that she wasn't in recovery, that she'd never touched an illegal substance in her life, but time reared forward too quickly. The buzz of the crowd blurred around them, disbelief changed to hurt on his face as the reporter's words sank in and he dropped her hand.

It was too late. She had no time to explain before he backed away, holding up his hands as if wanting nothing to do with her. She saw all her hopes plunge to the ground and shatter against the concrete.

Right along with her heart.

Chapter Fifteen

"She served a seven-year sentence. Didn't she tell you? Transporting an illegal substance across the border. Very serious charge." Tasha Brown's voice sounded tinny and distant, hardly noticeable above the thundering thud of his pulse in his ears. Liam shook his head, knocking away the last remnants of disbelief.

He'd let Brooke in, all the way in. He'd trusted her, the first woman he'd trusted since he'd been hurt. This wound? It cleaved all the way to his soul. His body rocked with pain so sharp his vision blurred. She stood there looking as innocent as ever. Sun gleaming in her long dark hair, delicate heart-shaped face, honest violet-blue eyes.

Not so honest. Not so innocent.

"You lied to me." The earth tipped and betrayal struck with a lethal blow. He fisted his hands and braced his feet, determined to hold on. "After what I told you, you knew."

"Just let me explain." The plea ardent in her eyes seemed to well up from the bottom of her entire being. For a moment he wanted to believe her, to believe in her, his sweet Brooke.

Then reason kicked in. He gave thanks for that. He'd been fooled once, but this was twice now. He thought of how gullible he'd been seeing only the good in her. How kind she'd been to Oscar, how beautiful she'd looked laughing in the May sunshine, how poignantly real with open heart and chaste kiss. He blew out a huff of air, frustrated with himself, angry with her and hurting. Just hurting.

"I told you about Sidney. You sympathized with me." The words had to be said. He hauled her by the wrist away from Tasha Brown, whose catlike grin had doubled. The instant his fingers closed around Brooke's slender wrist, emotion crashed through him like a tidal wave. Pure tenderness, complete sweetness and the love brimming from his soul he had to deny.

"You let me believe in you, but you are just like her." He dropped her wrist, pushed all the tenderness from his heart, crushed the love in his soul. "Day after day you made me think you were someone you weren't. Are you still using?"

"I never did." Wide eyes, trembling voice, she

gazed up at him like she'd been wounded to the core. "I promise you. It was a mistake."

"A mistake?" Like he could believe it. She had innocence down. He'd never seen a more convincing show. She was good. He had to give her that. "Funny, I've heard that before. We're done, Brooke."

"Wait, hear me out. I was driving up for a vacation in Canada. I was going to meet Darren there—"

"Don't bother. I don't want to hear your excuses. Seven years?" She was a convict. That pierced like a carving knife. Prison. She'd served a drug sentence. How could he not have seen that coming? Better question was, why hadn't he done a background search on her? He'd had the resources at the paper. He had to stop being such a trusting man. Disgusted, he stepped farther away from her. "I don't know you at all."

"Yes, you do. Everything I told you was true." Tears stood in her eyes, so convincing his anger almost faded.

Again. That woman had a hold on him. Praying for strength, he battled down the urge to lash out with words, words she probably deserved. But he wouldn't hurt her. He wasn't that kind of man.

"Caring for you was a mistake I intend to correct. We're done." He ground his teeth together, his jaw muscles jumped, his tendons corded tight in his neck. "Absolutely, positively done."

"Liam, I—" She watched him pivot on his heels, turning his back to her. Nothing hurt worse than watching him pound away. He didn't pause, he didn't look back. She didn't have to be a genius to know he'd meant what he said. She'd lost him.

For good.

"Brooke, I'm so sorry." Colbie's hand found hers and squeezed tight. "That was a terrible way for him to find out. I don't like that anchor lady."

All she could see was the blur of Liam merging with the crowd at the courthouse entrance. She blinked, realized she had tears in her eyes and willed them away. No crying allowed. She was stronger than that.

"Maybe you could talk to him." Brandi sidled up to hug Brooke. "He's a nice guy. I think he'll understand."

"No, he won't." He disappeared through the doors, gone from her sight. All she wanted was for him to come back. To turn around and realize there was no way the Brooke he'd fallen for could have hurt him or deceived him.

Please, she prayed. A tiny hope lived inside her and refused to budge. She clung to it with both hands, willing it to live. Wanting there to be some way to right this. But no tall, dark-haired man emerged through the throng and that small hope died. She bit down a sob and blinked harder against the rising tears she refused to let fall.

"We love you, Brooke." Bree sidled up to wrap her in another hug. Luke's hand landed on her shoulder. Hunter grunted in a reassuring, brotherly way. Lil gripped Brooke's hand, tears running down her face.

"I won't give up praying, dear." Lil held on so tight. "I could talk to Madge. There's got to be a way to fix this."

"Please don't." She leaned in to brush a kiss to Lil's appled cheek. "This is my fault. All mine. Promise me you won't bother him with this. He's hurt enough."

"So are you." Lil reached up to brush a tear away.

One had escaped. But no more. Brooke straightened her shoulders, steeled her resolve and took a deep, cleansing breath. *Lord, give me strength,* she prayed. Whatever it took, she had to put her broken heart aside, forget her shattered dreams and what might have been and concentrate on her sister. This was going to be another tough day for Bree.

That's why she was here. To support her sister. To be with her family.

She had to accept the fact that Liam was never meant to be hers.

It had been torture sitting in that courtroom. His whole being had collapsed in on itself like a black hole forming. Worse, he had a perfect view of Brooke up front, nestled between her sisters. Wherever he looked, there she was. At the corner of his eye. At the center of his view. The sheen of her glossy hair kept entering his field of vision as he watched Bree take the stand. The moment court adjourned for the day he hit the ground running, leaving a surprised Roger in his wake. No way did he want to risk bumping into Brooke, not when he was raw. Not when he felt like this.

He made a quick stop at the grocery store before swinging by to pick up Oscar. The moment the dog spotted him, he raced across the fenced playground in the Dillards' sunny backyard, barking in welcome. Chocolate eyes sparkled, doggy ears perked up—the animal hardly touched the ground. "Hello, hello, hello," he seemed to say as he bounced along, leaping happily.

"It's good to see you, too, buddy." He rubbed the Lab's head. At least he'd done something right.

The drive home was quick, with Oscar sniffing out the window. But not even the dog's presence could distract him from thinking of Brooke. He kept mulling over his mistakes, where he'd gone wrong and why he'd trusted her. The signs had been there. She'd been closed off; she'd been reluctant to open up. It was obvious now that she'd had secrets to hide.

A drug addict and trafficker. He just hadn't seen

that in her. He pulled into his driveway, shaking his head. He'd been caught up in her girl-next-door look and her wholesome act. Even now it was hard to believe.

Then again, he'd done the same thing with Sidney.

He stopped the truck in the driveway, cut the engine and sat in the shade. Without the bustle of court and the crowd around him and his errands done, he had a moment to just sit. The hurt he'd been fighting sank into him deeply. The dreams he'd had of her, dreams he'd wanted with her, blew away like dust spiraling in a heartless wind. All that was left was the void in his heart, deep and dark and agonizing.

He'd loved her. He hadn't realized how much until it was gone. Until he could measure the pain of her loss. His jaw clenched, his teeth ached from the pressure and he leaned farther back in his seat. A temperate wind breezed through the open window fanning his face, fragrant with the neighbor's lilacs and roses. The gray cat leaped into sight and perched on a fence post, watching them through slitted eyes.

How could I have done this again, Lord? He shook his head, unlatched his seat belt and grabbed his keys. He had no one to blame but himself. He was a reporter. If he'd been paying attention, did some research, maybe wondered why Tasha Brown had wanted to interview Brooke in the first place, he may have discovered her past sooner. Before she decimated his heart.

A weight settled on his shoulder. Oscar's chin. The Lab looked up at him with sympathetic eyes. Doggy brows arched with concern as if to say, "Are you all right?"

"No, but thanks, buddy." He leaned the side of his head against Oscar's, letting the moment be. The dog's comfort felt like a blessing. "You're all right, Oscar. Thanks for being my best friend."

A happy lick swiped across his chin. Liam chuckled. Funny guy. He straightened up, scrubbed the dog's ears. "Hey, you didn't even try to get into the grocery sacks."

Oscar sniffed the air, glanced at the bags on the front passenger seat and gave a toothy grin. All Oscar needed was to settle down and settle in. All he'd needed was a little love.

The quiet rumble of an engine pulled his attention. He glanced in his rearview and spotted Pop's sedan driving in behind him. Through the sunglinted glass, he caught his grandfather's smile. Their usual Friday night get-together was the best part of his week and he was grateful for it. Keeping busy was the key to not thinking about Brooke. To not feeling the wasteland his heart had become.

"Let's go say hi to Pop. What do you think?" he asked, and Oscar answered with a happy pant.

So he opened the door, hopped to the ground and waited for his dog to leap down.

"Hey, boy." Pop closed his car door, holding a paper sack. Looked like he'd stopped by the grocery store's bakery section on the way. "Liam, this is quite a dog you have here. What a good boy."

Hard to believe the Lab sat perfectly in front of Pop, waiting to be petted. And knowing Oscar, probably hoping for a bite of whatever treat was in that bag. "Yes, he's something, all right."

Oscar's tail whacked the concrete in happy agreement as he accepted a scrub on the top of his head from Pop and then took off, eagerly leading the way to the backyard gate, checking over his shoulder to make sure the humans were following him appropriately.

The cat on the fence watched the proceedings with mild interest.

"I've heard a rumor." Pop ambled up with a grin on his face.

"Oh, yeah?" He leaned across the truck seat to grab the two grocery bags. Paper crinkled as he straightened, shut the door and studied his grandfather. "What kind of rumor?"

"One about you." Pop's silver hair made him look distinguished and he stood straight and tall, just like always. "I heard from a few sources that you've been seen out and about with a pretty young lady."

So much for not thinking about Brooke. "Don't get your hopes up. She was just Oscar's trainer."

"I don't know. According to one source, you seemed like a great deal more."

"Maybe that was true once, but not now." He gathered up his defenses. He couldn't talk about this. He couldn't do it, no way. He opened the gate, Oscar leaped into his yard and the cat raised one paw and began washing his face.

"Oh. I had hopes for you, son." Pop frowned, disappointed, and closed the gate. "When I ran into Madge at Bible study, she told me all about you and one of the McKaslin girls."

"Gram is anxious to marry me off. She's reading way too much into things." Casual, that was the way to be. Maybe he could convince himself he wasn't in agony. That he didn't want to go back in time to this morning, when he was still with Brooke. When she was flawless in the morning sunshine, her laughter wrapping around his soul like a gift. When love filled him with possibilities and hopes.

Yes, he wanted that more than anything. But it could not be.

"Brooke's done helping Oscar, so that's the end of it." He shrugged, no big deal, even as he realized what he was doing. Covering up something that hurt him, so he wouldn't be as vulnerable and to protect himself. Talking about it would only hurt more.

No, he stopped the thought before it could start. That wasn't the same thing Brooke had done. She'd served time. She was not the sweet and honest woman he'd mistaken her for. He'd be smart not to start making excuses for her.

"Son, I've been praying for your heart to heal. You deserve to be happy again." Pop set his bakery bag on the patio table.

"Don't worry about me." He unlocked the kitchen door. "I'll be fine."

"That's debatable." Understanding layered Pop's baritone. "I saw how badly Sidney hurt you. Seems to me you're hurting like that again."

"No, this time it's worse." The truth tumbled out before he could stop it. He set the bags on the kitchen table and grabbed the matches from the junk drawer and a half-used bag of briquettes from the closet.

"I'm sorry to hear that, son." Pop tugged the barbecue away from the side of the house. "I've been praying for you. I want you to know the wonder and sanctuary of love."

"I'm disillusioned. More than disillusioned." Love leads to heartbreak. He'd known that all along. He waited for Pop to remove the steel lid of the grill before upending the bag. Chunks of charcoal tumbled. Why was he remembering the first evening Brooke had come over, after Oscar had disheveled the house? He'd been intending to barbecue that night, too.

"Don't let anything harden your heart." Pop se the rack in place. Concern shaped his distinguished features. "The years I spent with your grandmother were the best in my life. She was taken from me too soon, but I know if she were here she would want me to tell you—don't give up on love."

"I appreciate the message, but I'm done with love. Finished." He rolled up the bag and reached for the lighter fluid. He couldn't explain why Brooke had gotten so far in that she owned a piece of his soul. That was one puzzle he wasn't going to pursue. He didn't need the answer to it. He needed it to go away. To cease being. For God to wipe the memory of Brooke McKaslin from his brain.

Oscar's bark interrupted his thoughts.

"Look at that goofy dog. He brightens things up doesn't he?" Pop chuckled, already enamored.

"He sure does." Oscar trotted alongside the fence, trailing the cat who was skimming the top boards, tossing a Cheshire cat look over his shoulder. Besotted, Oscar followed, hoping to be friends

But the brightness was only temporary. Liam didn't know how he was going to get past his all consuming grief, the worst he'd ever known. He li a match and dropped it. Watched the flame catch and fire spread. Brooke was a dream that had never been real.

But it sure had felt like it could have been. He shook his head, huffed out a breath and wished he could stop his soul from bleeding.

Chapter Sixteen

A pervasive misery gripped her, refusing to let go. Nothing seemed to loosen that hopeless feeling. Not working with Kerry Linton's sweet old dog, and not running errands for Colbie and helping around the house. Not even heading out Sunday after church with Luke and Hunter to see their dairy farm in the peaceful Montana countryside. No matter what she did the weight of what she'd done and the harm she'd caused lurked, refusing to budge.

As long as she lived, she would never forget the hurt carved on Liam's face when he'd walked away from her. In protecting herself, she'd harmed him. She unrolled the bag of pancake mix, measured it into a mixing bowl and listened to her movements rustle in the trailer's cozy kitchen. Sunrise painted pink across the eastern landscape. Ethereal golden

un shone upon the new day like hope. Like a re-
ssurance that heaven wasn't as far away as it felt.

She hadn't meant to hurt him, but it didn't matter
now. The way he'd avoided glancing her way in
ourt and how he'd taken off immediately after the
ession last week. Probably he'd be the same way
n court today. She couldn't blame him. She opened
he fridge and hauled out the carton of milk. She
new exactly how hard betrayal could scar.

"Just what do you think you're doing?" Colbie
urst into the kitchen fresh from the shower, her
ong hair still wet.

"Making breakfast for my family." The measur-
ng cup clanked to the counter and she scooped a
vooden spoon out of a drawer. "Don't think I don't
now what you're up to."

"How do you know it was me?" Colbie dug out
fry pan from a bottom cabinet.

"Who else would leave a brochure from the local
echnical college next to the couch where I was
leeping?" She gave the batter a few good stirs. "I
lidn't know they had a veterinary assistant pro-
ram nearby."

"Funny what a little investigative work will turn
p." Colbie thunked the pan onto the burner. "You
ould stay here or with the twins. The next time
here's an opening at the bookstore, I'll get you on.
can do that, you know, since I'm the manager. Or,
ven better, I know the receptionist at Dr. Flynn's

office, a veterinarian from our church, and I'm per
suasive. I might be able to get you a job there, yo
know, answering phones or cleaning up. Somethin
entry-level."

"Colbie, stop." Her lovely sister, so determine
to right wrongs. "You have to stop trying to fix m
past. It's over."

"I can't help it. I like to fix things." She grabbe
a carton of eggs from the fridge. "This is my las
bid since you're leaving tomorrow. I know you'v
got that interview, but I have to say it—pleas
stay."

I wish. That thought rose up through the shard
of her heart like a new dream taking flight. She le
go of the spoon and leaned back against the coun
ter.

"We want you here." Love drove Colbie—i
was plain to see now. That was her only motive
"I know Montana has bad memories for you, bu
maybe it can have even better ones, too. Mayb
everything you really want is right here. Liam i
here."

"You know how things turned out with Liam.
She spun away to hide the grimace of pain. Sh
tugged open the fridge and got out orange juic
jelly, maple syrup. The bottles plunked on th
counter in a determined rhythm as she fough
not to think about the man. About his check tha
had arrived in Lil's box with the Saturday mai

No note, just a generous check, considering the number of hours she'd put in with Oscar.

Not that she intended to cash it. Ever. She'd torn it up into tiny bits and tossed it in the kitchen garbage can. She couldn't accept pay, not after how she'd hurt him. It felt like pay-off money, a check he'd written just to get rid of the bad memories she'd left with him.

"You should try to explain." Colbie leaned in to grab a package of bacon from the shelf. "Liam will understand. He'll forgive you."

"No, he won't." She'd never forget the look on his face. It was over. He despised her. What were the chances anything could change that?

None, that's what. It couldn't have worked from the beginning. She had no one to blame but herself. And Liam? He'd been the innocent one. It wasn't right and it wasn't fair that he'd gotten hurt.

A muted thud sounded from the front porch. Colbie looked up from peeling strips of bacon from the pack. "The morning paper. Would you mind fetching it? You know how Mom likes to read it over breakfast."

"I do." She pushed away from the counter, glad to get a little air. The pressure inside her chest made it tough to breathe in the little kitchen. It felt good to yank open the door and step into the peaceful morning.

The newspaper, rolled up and rubber-banded, sat

on the far corner of the little porch. Lark song serenaded her as she padded across the sunny boards, breathing in the freshness. Overhead the canopy of leafy trees fluttered as they reached for the blue sky. The last lilac blooms of the season sent fragrance her way. She gripped the wooden rail and breathed it in.

Memories of being a girl playing beneath big skies and rolling hills rose up, reminding her of who she used to be. Who she was always meant to be. Darren's betrayal, the jury's decision and those years locked away behind bars had never been God's plan for her. She could feel that on the touch of the wind against her face.

Colbie was right. She couldn't let the past diminish her future. This was her life, the one God had given her. It was up to her to make the best of it, come what may. She'd been through hard times, but they didn't have to keep holding her back. They didn't have to determine who she would become. That was her choice.

"Brooke, is that you?" Madge Jones squinted from her flowerbed, extricating her morning paper from the rose bush where it had apparently fallen. "I hear you're leaving on the bus in the morning. Lil says you got some fancy interview."

"Not unless you call minimum wage fancy."

"Too bad. I got another job all lined up for you. The neighbor on the other side of me has a biting

Pekinese. Nearly took my toes off when I was over there." She straightened, shook leaves off her paper and squinted. "Funny you haven't asked me how Oscar and Liam are doing."

"I, uh—" Words failed her. She shifted, ashamed, wondering how much Madge knew. Was she aware how hard she'd fallen for Liam? That no matter how hard she tried, the affection—*no, time to be honest, Brooke*—actually, love she felt would not end? It remained in broken pieces of her heart she could not fix. Did Madge know how she'd hurt him?

"His surgery's this afternoon," Madge went on. "Ridiculous if you ask me."

"S-surgery?" The word tore from her. She tumbled down the steps, hardly breathing. "What happened? What's wrong?"

"As if taking in that dog wasn't enough, now Liam's got a vet bill." Madge shook her head, the layer of concern in her voice gentling her words.

"It's Oscar." For a brief instant she'd thought it was Liam. That something had happened to him. She sagged against the handrail and sank onto the bottom step. Her pulse cannoned in her ears and boomed against her ribs. She covered her face with her hands, shaking hard.

"I don't know what all that costs, but I can tell you, it's a pretty penny." Madge unwound the rubber band, tucked it into her apron pocket and shook out the newsprint. "Liam has been talking me into getting a little house dog, but after what he's been through with that one, I put my foot down."

"That's not a little wistfulness I hear, is it?" She lowered her hands.

"Not even close." But a little smile tugged at the corners. Madge frowned, attempting to hide it. Her gaze sharpened, all gentleness gone. Perhaps she knew what had happened after all.

"Is Oscar going to be okay?" She had to know. "Nothing terrible happened or you would have told me, right?"

"Oh, he has a tumor in his leg. Liam took him running last Saturday morning and the dog was limping afterward." Madge inched closer, a woman on a mission. "Dr. Flynn took a look and did an ultrasound and a needle biopsy. They should get the lab results in a few days. Meanwhile, he's scheduled for surgery this afternoon."

"Poor Oscar." She shook too hard to think of standing. Her heart broke all over again. She loved that dog. Absolutely, positively loved him. Tears prickled behind her eyes. A sob gathered in her throat.

"As I hear it, you were the one who noticed it in the first place." Madge's penetrating gaze didn't stop, as if she were trying to say something with that look. "I suppose you'd want to stop by. Surgery starts at two o'clock. It's the clinic off Vista

Way. Oh, here come the twins driving up. I hope all goes well on the stand for Bree today. You tell her I'll be praying for her."

"I will. Thanks, Mrs. Jones." She took a shaky breath, prayed her knees would hold her and pushed off the step.

Bree's little pickup rumbled into the gravel parking strip, idling roughly. The engine sputtered to a stop, doors flung open and the twins popped out, ready for court. Bree looked so grown up in her dark suit and white blouse. Her heels wobbled in the grass until she made it to the walkway. Strong, lovely, mature. She seemed ready to take on the court and the entire world. "Brooke. We hate this is the last morning…"

"…we'll be able to see you," Brandi finished, circling around the far side of the pickup. Equally as lovely in trim trousers and a blue blouse, she hurried to catch up with her sister. "I don't know how we're going let you go tomorrow."

"Neither do I." She might as well admit it. Leaving was going to hurt. She held out her arms. "Group hug."

"Group hug." Colbie poked her nose out the door, gave the screen door a push and tumbled into the morning, spatula in hand. "Here's to the McKaslin sisters. One for all and all for one."

"Amen to that." Brooke pulled her sisters close.

The sun chose that moment to rise above the trees
casting them in a golden light. As if heaven shined
down on them, too.

"You did a great job, Brianna." The distinct at
torney rose from his chair the moment the gavel
hit. The closing arguments were done and the
jury's deliberation would begin. Handsome Austin
Quinn managed a grave but hopeful twist to his
mouth, somewhere between a frown and a grin
"You made a great difference today."

"Oh, I think that's what you did. I just told the
truth." Bree reached out to take Max's hand and
the way their gazes met spoke of everlasting love
With this hard episode behind her, Bree could look
forward to planning her wedding. It was like sun
shine after a storm, dawn after a long night and
Brooke felt encouraged as she helped Colbie scoo
Lil's chair around in the aisle.

Was it her imagination or was Austin Quinn
looking her way? Brooke glanced over her shoul
der, bumped into Colbie and caught the distric
attorney's head turning away fast. He'd been
watching Colbie, she realized. Pretty and adorable
Colbie. Her stomach sank as she watched Austin
cross the courtroom, back straight, shoulders set
No doubt a lot of nice men noticed Colbie, but
every one of them walked away.

"I don't know about anyone else, but I need ic

cream." Colbie, unaware of what had happened, gave her mom's hand a loving squeeze. "Is anyone else with me?"

"Me!" Brandi, the first to volunteer, stumbled into the aisle.

"Me," Bree spoke up, her hand twined with Max's. "I need chocolate. Lots and lots of chocolate. Bring it on."

"Don't look at me." Hunter stalked over to Colbie and nudged her out of the way, determined to take charge of Lil's chair. "I don't eat that stuff. I'm afraid it will make me sweet."

"We can't have that." Brooke couldn't resist teasing, even with Liam on her mind. "You're already way too sweet as it is."

Taciturn Hunter frowned, giving Lil's chair a good push, and everyone chuckled. It felt like a welcome relief after the stress and sadness of the trial.

"I'm in for ice cream," Luke said, taking the lead. "I'm sweet but I could always be sweeter."

"That's your problem," Hunter scoffed, fighting a grin, fighting to stay gruff. "You're too soft."

"Aw, but women like men with tender hearts," Luke bantered back.

"Funny thing is, I don't see any women around you but family. And the way I see it, they're stuck with you." Hunter winked.

"Sure, I might be in a dating dry spell but at least

I don't scare 'em off." Luke winked, protecting Brandi and Colbie from the shuffle of the crowd.

"Scare 'em? I run 'em off on purpose," Hunter growled, full well knowing it would make everyone chuckle.

She didn't want to miss the post-trial ice cream celebration. This was her last day with her family, her last day in Montana. Her stomach twisted in knots. She'd felt Liam's presence in the back of the room during the morning session. She'd been aware of him like a touch to her spirit, like music in her soul and the moment he'd slipped out at noon, her spirit had gone dark. Her soul silent.

She'd hurt him. She couldn't live with that but she couldn't go on until she did the right thing.

"Brooke, I have some of that special no-calorie ice cream." Colbie glanced over her shoulder. "You're coming, too, right?"

"No, I commandeered Bree's pickup for a reason." She glanced at her phone's screen. 2:25 p.m. She drew in a rattling breath, gathering her courage. This wasn't going to be easy. "There's someplace I need to be."

Chapter Seventeen

How did this happen? In the vet's waiting room, Liam leaned forward in the chair and pressed the heel of his hand to his forehead. How could his heart possibly be this shredded? Get a dog, he'd thought when the lonely evenings rattling around his house had gotten to him. It had seemed like a great idea at the time. He wanted a companion, a buddy, nothing more, nothing that would shatter his heart.

Too late for that. The pieces of his heart that Brooke had broken were now being shredded into smaller bits by Oscar. Not exactly his plan in life. The Bible verse about man making many plans but the Lord's will prevailing jumped into his head. He launched out of the chair, feeling foolish. He'd never been in charge of his heart.

A car door closed in the parking lot, muffled by the row of windows. Awareness moved through his soul. He knew it was Brooke before he saw her round the front of the old pickup. Hurt and bitterness squeezed hard in his chest, but it wasn't strong enough to shadow the pure love within him. It shone a beam of light through the deepest darkness.

Just let her go, he told himself. He didn't want to love a woman like that. One who moved through the May day like a sunbeam, her hair fluttering in the breeze. One so beautiful and kind, he'd been blinded by it. He'd let himself think for one brief moment she was real, that his dreams for her could be real, too.

Their gazes locked through the window. He ignored the rock to his heart, the jolt. He refused to acknowledge the apology poignant in those violet-blue depths and softening her rosebud mouth. Snapping to attention, he held himself tight and turned his back, set against her. Every muscle tensed, his resolve firm and his stance unyielding.

Seconds ticked by, each as long as eternity until the door opened and she tapped in. He felt the touch of her gaze on his back and sensed her hesitation. Silence stretched between them, but he didn't intend to break it. He hadn't invited her here. He didn't want to hear her excuses. As hard as it was to believe, he'd finally seen the woman she was. A liar. Someone pretending to be what she wasn't.

"L-Liam?" Her alto wobbled, the perfect pitch to portray vulnerability. "How's Oscar?"

"The last I heard his surgery is going fine." *Be tough,* he told himself. *Don't turn around. Don't look at her.* "Still don't know if it's cancer or not."

"I'm so sorry." Sorrow laced her words. An award-winning actress couldn't have topped her portrayal. She padded closer and he ignored the tug of his soul toward her, held by some unexplained gravitational pull that defied logic. She laid a hand to his arm, the lightest brush and brief. "Is there anything I can do?"

He wanted to be harsh. He wanted to order her away, but his arm tingled where she'd touched it and that innocent sensation of pure emotion arrowed all the way to the broken pieces of him. This would be easier if she wasn't kind. If she were as cold and selfish as Sidney, a woman who only cared about getting what she wanted, then the solution would be easy. He'd just tell her to leave.

But she stood right where he could see the tremendous worry crinkling in the corners of her eyes, so honest even he started to believe it.

Fine, she cared about Oscar. But that didn't mean he had to give an inch. He cleared his throat so when he spoke, no emotion showed. "I'd prefer to wait alone, if you don't mind. I can have Dr. Flynn's receptionist call you when Oscar's out of surgery."

"Thanks." Disappointment weighed down her

voice, but he didn't want to analyze it. He no longer cared about figuring out Brooke McKaslin. She bit her bottom lip, worrying it while she debated. "I couldn't leave town not knowing how he was. I have something for him."

He clamped his teeth together. He listened to the whisper of her purse flap, the rustle of paper and the scent of vanilla as she moved in. She held out a wrapped gift. "I thought he deserved a present after what he's been through."

"Thanks." He hated accepting it because he had to turn and get the full impact of her. The silent plea in her eyes, the sorrow on her face, the question unspoken in her heart. He could feel that question as if it were a part of him. He didn't know how to stop the connection he felt with her or how to protect himself against it. "I'm sure Oscar will appreciate it."

"There's one more thing." She clasped her hands together. They were obviously trembling. "I owe you an apology."

"Don't worry about it." He waved her concerns away. He didn't need to hear them. The shredded remnants of his heart tore even more until he couldn't stand it. "It's the past. It's over. No need to drag it up."

"No, it's not. I hurt you. I kept the truth from you and that's as good as a lie." She winced, her brightness dimming as if wrapped in shame. "I'm sorry."

"I don't need your apology." It hurt too much. He'd believed in her. Watching her in the park with Oscar, laughing with her in the morning sunshine, feeling like she was a kindred spirit. It remained, taunting him. "Maybe it's better if you just go now."

"Sure, but I c-can't." Tears stood in her eyes, genuine.

Genuine? He shook his head. He couldn't start believing her.

"I know what it feels like to trust someone and have them betray you. It cripples your ability to trust the next person who comes along, someone who might be good for you." She blew out a shaky breath, then bit her lip again as if fighting for courage and the right words. "I don't want that for you. I don't want you to think I've hurt you the way Sidney did and to close your heart to love."

"Don't worry about it." He turned away, acting casual, fighting to keep her words from touching him.

"I don't want to be responsible for that, Liam. You are a good man. I know. After Darren, I wasn't going to trust anyone. Not a single man. Then you came along and I couldn't help it. You were good and kind and wonderful. I just fell for you. There wasn't one thing I could do about it and I tried. Believe me."

That's how it had been for him, too. Even now he

struggled as hard as he could to hold back the tide of affection threatening to let loose with tsunami force.

"I didn't tell you about prison because I was afraid to. It would change how you saw me, and I didn't want that. Not after you told me about Sidney."

"You would rather let me believe a lie."

"I tried to get my courage up, but I didn't do it quickly enough." She came closer, radiating enough pain that even he could feel it. "I told you about Darren. What I didn't say was how he asked me to meet his grandparents, who lived in Vancouver. I thought he was going to propose to me because I was finally meeting the people most important to him growing up."

"And did you?" Nothing was going to move him. Not her story or her quiet sincerity. Not the wobble of her chin or the misery shadowing her eyes. No, he was stone. Cold, unfeeling stone.

"No. He was going to meet me at his grandparents' home. He had some traveling to do for work." Her knees shook, so she eased down into a nearby chair. Her dark hair tumbled around her face like a shield. "He put a few things in my car's trunk for me to take along. A duffel bag, a few grocery sacks. I didn't look in them. I figured it was his hockey stuff and gifts for his grandparents."

"But it wasn't?"

"Not even close." She shook her head, fisting her hands to hold back the pain of betrayal that still cut like a blade. "I drove right up to the Canadian border checkpoint, so happy I could hardly contain myself. I was already planning our wedding— that is, until the border agents found drugs in my trunk."

"Supposedly Darren's, huh?" He glared down at her, his blue depths remote. He set aside Oscar's gift, turning away from her.

Staring at the broad plane of his back, she'd never felt so small. So alone. Bereft, she fought to find the right words and the strength to say them.

"I didn't know what it was at first. I'd never seen heroin or anything like it. At first I couldn't believe what was happening." Once again she could feel the clasp of the handcuffs around her wrist and the panic roaring through her. Remembering was tearing her apart. "I tried to explain, but they wouldn't believe me. The federal agents called in wouldn't believe me, either. Not even my court-appointed defense attorney thought I was telling the truth."

"Maybe because you were caught red-handed?" His words rang harshly, but something softened in his eyes. She feared it was pity.

"I wasn't that dumb. If I had been transporting drugs, I wouldn't have tried driving through a checkpoint at the border where they look for things like that." What had been obvious to her had not been plain to the jury. "I went to federal prison with women who had committed terrible crimes. Nothing was more terrifying. I lost my friends, my life as I knew it, my hope for going to school. And Darren? He never called. He never visited. He didn't show for my trial. Two years later he was arrested for transporting heroin. He's still in jail."

"Some might say you were in it together." He folded his hands across his chest, a barrier between them, one impossible to scale.

She hadn't come to try to change his mind. She'd already lost him. There was no way to fix that. She lifted her chin. "I know the truth. You believe what you want. But I want to know I've done what I can to set this right. So you won't carry around a sense of betrayal that you don't need to. Believe me—it wasn't easy to come here."

"No." He watched everything about her. Her raw emotions written on her face, so dark in her eyes he couldn't see anything but integrity as she rose from the chair. A woman who put her life together after injustice tore it apart. No wonder her family was protective of her, no wonder Colbie kept looking after her.

"Take good care of yourself, Liam." Unguarded, there was no more mystery. He could see all the way to her soul. He could see the woman who didn't believe love could happen to her. Or that someone outside her family could see the truth.

She took a shivery breath, popped out of her chair and swished away so quickly he couldn't think fast enough to stop her. Apology weighed down her voice as she glanced over her shoulder. "It changed my life knowing you. Goodbye."

"I—" The words clumped in his throat, a tangle of emotion and affection he couldn't get past his Adam's apple. Maybe because he was afraid to say them. Tender words did not come easily to him and he needed them now. He needed to move past his comfort zone and put his heart on the line.

"Liam?" Dr. Flynn startled him, coming up on his blind side. He swung toward her and in the partial second that he took his focus off Brooke, he heard the door whisper open. He felt her presence slip away. When he looked back, the door swung shut. All he could see of Brooke was a flash in the window rushing down the sidewalk, taking every scrap of his heart with her.

"Oscar made it through surgery just fine," Dr. Flynn informed him. "The tumor was small and localized. I feel confident I got it all. We'll hear from pathology maybe late tomorrow or the next day. He's in recovery right now. You can see him in an hour or so."

"Thanks." Relief crashed through him and he was grateful for the encouraging news, but all he could think of was Brooke. He couldn't forget the apology in her eyes, the thin and traumatized sound of her voice as she told her story and the bleak grief written on her lovely face. She was the woman who could have been the love of his life.

She collapsed behind the wheel, plugged in the key and that was as far as she got before the agony overwhelmed her. At least she'd kept it together in front of him. That was what mattered. She choked on a mangled sob, forced it back down and covered her face with her hands. Apologizing to him had been one of the toughest things she'd had to do in a long while. He hadn't believed her. She'd read it on his face. All the time they'd spent together, the moments they'd shared, it hadn't been enough for him to believe in her.

Maybe it never would have. The sob trapped in her chest expanded, becoming a well of grief. See what a bad idea falling in love was? She'd fought it, she'd denied it, she'd done everything she could to stop it and even now, when all hope was lost, she loved him with a depth that had no end.

Just breathe in and out, she told herself. *Breathe in fresh air, breathe out pain.* This would pass. She had to accept this was God's will. She wanted to be obedient to His path for her, but losing Liam hurt. It would always hurt. The gentleness of his love was the sweetest thing she'd ever known.

The sun beaming through the glass heated up the truck, so she rolled down the window, cranking away. Soothing summer breezes fanned her damp cheeks and she swiped away the tears she hadn't remembered crying. One painful thing down, one more left to do. Time to head back to Colbie and Lil's and pack. How was she going to say goodbye to her family? Tears blurred her eyes and she blinked them away furiously. What was wrong with her? Why was she falling apart?

Because her barriers were gone, the shutters surrounding her heart dismantled. She sat utterly defenseless, reeling from a lethal blow. It felt as if once again her life was in shambles, nothing but pieces impossible to put together.

"Brooke?" Liam emerged from the bright glare of the sunlight, pacing toward her. Powerful shoulders, confident stride, gorgeous man. He stalked toward her like a soldier on a mission, shoes striking the concrete with an intensity that made her breath catch.

She rubbed away all signs of damp from her cheeks and snapped straight up in the seat. No way did she want him to see her falling apart like this. She would be okay. She had a plan in place. She would head home—not home, to Colbie and Lil's—and pack. Have a farewell supper with the family. Leave on the morning bus. She shoved flyaway hair out of her eyes, watching as Liam stepped off the curb, so close she could see the muscle jump along his jaw.

Was he mad at her? Had he come for closure, too? To say what he had to so he could let go of her forever? Air swished out of her lungs in a little gasp. She lifted her chin, determined to listen to whatever he needed to say.

"Oscar's going to be okay." He stopped beside the truck, all six foot plus of him, windblown and so incredible her spirit leaned toward his against her will.

"Good news." Just what she needed. She relaxed back into the seat. Liam didn't look ready to confront her, but he didn't look pleased to be talking with her, either. She studied his face, set in stone, and his granite eyes. So distant. She didn't blame him one bit. She blew out another breath, glad about Oscar's surgery. "You must be relieved."

"I am." He didn't look it. He looked so remote he could have been a statue hewn from marble, chiseled with a craftsman's skill. His jaw ground, as if he were debating what to say. "You can't just walk away like that. You didn't give me a chance to tell you what I think."

"I already know." She winced. With no shields to put up, she had no way to protect herself from what he was about to say. How could she endure hearing how he was glad she'd be leaving because he wanted nothing to do with her ever again?

"No, I don't think you know exactly how upset I am." He splayed both hands on the side of the truck, peering in at her through the open window. His sky-blue eyes bored into her with the intensity of a high-powered laser. "I'm upset at myself."

"What?" That made no sense. Not at all.

"You didn't feel safe enough with me to show me your vulnerable side, what's hurt you in your life." His granite gaze softened, gentleness shining blue as dreams. "That story you told me in there. That was a lot to go through."

"It knocked me down good for a while, but I got through it." When would he finally let out his anger at her? she wondered. When would he finally tell her exactly what he thought of her?

"You never got to hear my opinion." He pulled open the door, eliminating the only barrier between them, the only one she had. Exposed, she gazed up at him.

"I've been around the globe reporting on everything." He leaned in, planted one hand on the dash and the other on the seat back beside her. "I've heard enough to know the truth when I hear it."

"What?" Surely she hadn't heard him right. That couldn't be. Even her own mother hadn't believed her. She simply wanted his forgiveness so badly she was making it up in her head.

"I'm sorry you went through that, beautiful." He brushed a spray of flyaway tendrils out of her eyes, his touch more tender than anything she'd known before. "I can't imagine how tough that had to be. And I'm sorry."

"You believe me?" She blinked up at him, unconvinced.

"I do." His hand cupped the side of her face, his skin warmly comforting against her cheek. "Because I see you, Brooke. All of you. Your heart is an open book to me. I can see right in. Do you know why?"

She shook her head, emotions and words too tangled up inside her to speak.

"Because I love you. I really love you." Nothing was more honest than the rumble of his words. "I promise I'll be a safe place for you from now on. My heart is on the line, Brooke. Is there a chance that you feel this way for me, too?"

Lord, is this what You have in store for me? Love? Tears broke forth like a dam, washing away all the hard times, all the disillusion and pain, leaving only hope. Hope that rose up as if with angels' wings because he loved her.

The deepest affection twisted through her, plowing through her pain, unstoppable, shining so bright it was all she could see. "I love you, Liam. More than words can say."

She laid her hand on his, cherishing the masculine comfort of his touch, grateful for the connection between them, one that strengthened with each breath, each heartbeat. She watched relief move across his face and commitment take root in his soul.

"We can do this long distance if you want," he said, easing onto his knees. "But I would rather that you stayed nearby so I can see your beautiful face every day. Marry me, Brooke. I want to be your happily-ever-after."

"I want to be yours. Yes, I'd love to marry you." She flew into his arms, the safest haven on earth. She held him so tight, as tightly as he held her. She couldn't believe she was tucked against his chest, listening to the thump of his heart, about to become his wife. His wife!

As if he felt the same, he brushed tender kisses to the top of her head and the side of her face. When she lifted her cheek from his chest she saw the ardent devotion shining in those depths of blue. The kind of love she'd always dreamed about.

His kiss was flawless and gentle, full of heart. Everything a kiss should be. The sun chose that moment to brighten, as if heaven gave its approval. She remembered to thank God as she sank against Liam's chest, nestling into his arms, home at last.

Epilogue

Late June, one month later

Evening sun peered over the stand of tall evergreens bordering the trailer park as Brooke McKaslin stepped foot outside. A hot burst of breeze met her on Lil's back patio where chaos reigned. In the fenced yard, Hunter and Luke manned the barbecue, aided by Max, offering his advice.

Lil in her wheelchair rested in the shade by the picnic table, reading a paperback book. Colbie and the twins waged a squirt gun war at the edge of the lawn, their happy squeals adding to the merriment as Oscar barked, racing at their heels. Bree sited and shot, laughing merrily. With the trial behind her and the Backdoor Burglars convicted, she and Max had set a Christmas wedding.

All was well in the McKaslin world. Brooke shifted the tray balanced in both hands so she could shove the screen door shut, but something stopped her. A sneaker wedged in the doorjamb, belonging to a hulking shadow that became Liam. Tall, striking and hers. His sky-blue eyes hooked her, soul-deep.

"Hey, gorgeous." He ambled through the door, leaning in like a man on a mission. A mission she did not intend to thwart.

His lips brushed hers slow and gentle. She could feel his heart and his devotion in that kiss. So beautiful, she didn't want it to end. When he broke away, the depths of his heart shone in his eyes. Every time she saw it, it took her breath away. His deep and abiding affection was more precious than anything she'd known before.

"Sometimes love leads to a miracle," he murmured low, so only she could hear. "It led me to you."

She'd made the right decision staying in town. After canceling her interview she'd let Colbie talk Dr. Flynn into a part-time job for her. She'd enrolled in a vet assistant program starting fall quarter. The diamond ring on her hand sparkled with the same brilliance her life had become. Jogging every morning with Liam and Oscar—his tumor had been benign—volunteering at the youth center and barbecuing in Liam's backyard. Each moment spent with her fiancé was the happiest of her life. A dream come true she thanked God for over and over again.

"Oscar!" Hunter's shout thundered through the yard. "Get back here with that hot dog! Bad dog!"

His words held no sting as laughter erupted in the backyard. A golden blur reached the middle of the lawn, a safe distance away from the men at the grill, and all four paws skidded to a stop. Doggy ears perked, apologetic brows arched over chocolate eyes and Oscar glanced around as if he couldn't quite believe it had happened again. The food thief inside him had taken over. He seemed surprised to notice the hot dog clenched between sharp teeth.

"Give that back." Hunter tossed down his barbecue tongs, stalking toward the culprit.

Oscar seemed unrepentant as he chomped down and swallowed. The hot dog disappeared. As Hunter approached Oscar offered a toothy grin and the equivalent of a canine shrug as if to say, "Oops."

"Who trained this dog?" Hunter growled, shaking his head. "You did a terrible job, Brooke."

"I never said I trained him perfectly." She set the tray on the picnic table, laughing. These days she was always laughing. "But you're perfect just the way you are, aren't you, Oscar?"

Big brown eyes glittered in agreement.

"That's the word. Perfect." Liam's arms wrapped around her from behind and they watched the scene together. Brandi called to Oscar and tossed him a pongy ball. Colbie squirted Bree with her water ifle. Hunter went back to the grill to talk farm-ng with the guys. And Lil watched with a happy mile. The back gate opened and Liam's grandfa-her ambled in. He held the gate for Madge, who'd een invited to dinner, too.

"Yes, our life is absolutely perfect," she agreed. 'And it's going to get better and better. With you, Liam, I couldn't ask for anything more."

The future stretched ahead so bright it hurt the ye to see. Home was the best place to be. Luke an-ounced the food was ready, everyone took a plate nd they gathered together, all of them, a family.

* * * * *

Dear Reader,

Returning to the McKaslin Clan stories has been like coming home for me, writing about the family I love most. I hope you feel that way, too, when you turn the pages of this book and find old friends in the McKaslins. This time it's Brooke's story—the prodigal sister returns home as the family gathers around Brianna to support her through her testimony as a witness. Brooke has plans to leave once the trial is over—no way does she want to stay in Montana where the past can haunt her. So when she meets Liam Knightly and his dog, Oscar, the last thing she expects is for her life to change or for God to nudge her slowly but surely in the direction He means her to go.

I hope you are carried away by Brooke's romance, you laugh out loud with Oscar's antics and you are reminded of all the kinds of love that come into a person's life—and what great blessings they are.

Thank you for choosing *Montana Homecoming* and for returning to the McKaslin family with me.

As always, wishing you love and peace,

Jillian Hart

Questions for Discussion

1. What are your first impressions of Brooke? How would you describe her?

2. What are your first impressions of Liam? How does he interact with his dog? What does this tell you about his character?

3. What do you think of Oscar? What role does he play in the story? Have you ever known a dog like Oscar?

4. What secret do you think Brooke is hiding? What do you think happened to her in the past?

5. What do you think Brooke feels when she learns Liam is a reporter? Would you feel this way, too? Why does it push them apart?

6. How did Brooke's arrest and conviction affect her?

7. Family and friends speculate and meddle in Brooke and Liam's relationship. What part do they play in the budding romance? How does this affect Brooke? Liam?

8. What makes Brooke soften her stance against Liam? How does he affect her? What does she learn about Liam?

9. What are Liam's strengths? What are his weaknesses? What do you come to admire about him?

10. What values do you think are important in this book?

11. What do you think are the central themes in this book? How do they develop? What meanings do you find in them?

12. In the beginning of the story, Brooke wrestles with the losses resulting from her mistake of trusting the wrong man. What does she learn by the end of the story? What has she learned about life? About where God is leading her?

13. How does God guide both Brooke and Liam? How is this evident? How does God lead them to true love?

14. There are many different kinds of love in this book. What are they? What does Brooke learn about true love?

Love Inspired®
SUSPENSE
RIVETING INSPIRATIONAL ROMANCE

Watch for our series of edge-
of-your-seat suspense novels.
These contemporary tales
of intrigue and romance
feature Christian characters
facing challenges to their faith...
and their lives!

AVAILABLE IN REGULAR
& LARGER-PRINT FORMATS